Guns and Dreamers

Jason McKinney feels the need to explore and decides to head out on his own to see the country beyond Kansas. When his offer of help is declined by a couple of bounty hunters he tries to hook up with in Wichita, Jason makes the decision to head south. Upon his return from an eye-opening but short-lived venture into Texas, he finds his father, Mac Shepard, is now a wanted man. With Mac on the run, Jason is reluctantly forced to take charge of the ranch while his nearest neighbour schemes to take full possession.

By the same author

Bitter is the Dust

Guns and Dreamers

Scott Gese

A Black Horse Western

ROBERT HALE

© Scott Gese 2017
First published in Great Britain 2017

ISBN 978-0-7198-2395-4

The Crowood Press
The Stable Block
Crowood Lane
Ramsbury
Marlborough
Wiltshire SN8 2HR

www.bhwesterns.com

Robert Hale is an imprint
of The Crowood Press

Typeset by
Derek Doyle & Associates, Shaw Heath
Printed and bound in Great Britain by
CPI Group (UK) Ltd, Croydon, CR0 4YY

CHAPTER 1

NEW BEGINNINGS

Miles Hanley was about as furious as a man could be and still maintain some control. After what had occurred, he considered Sheriff Mason to be no more than a lazy son-of-a-bitch and his deputies inept. They had all ridden off without checking anything beyond Mac Shepard's empty corrals. Why on God's green earth would any man in his right mind put stolen cattle in his own corral? *He wouldn't,* thought Miles; and that's why the corrals were empty. Mason should have known that. Maybe he did. In any case, the lawman and his men had left Miles to pursue Mac Shepard on his own.

The earlier confrontation with Shepard may not have produced a live cow, but he *had* heard the train, and the smell of fresh cow shit still hung heavy in the air. Besides, he had known for certain there had been close to two hundred head in the area shortly before he arrived. His men had seen them with their own eyes; and there were still plenty of signs. Hell, a blind man could have seen the milling tracks of cloven hoofs, and certainly would have sensed the fresh droppings that littered the otherwise flat ground.

Mac Shepard may not have rustled the cows himself, but that sure in hell didn't mean he hadn't hired someone to do it for him. As far as Miles was concerned, that was the same as Mac stealing them himself. And even though the cattle didn't belong to Miles, nor were they on his property, in his own way of thinking he considered what had taken place that evening a hanging offense just the same.

Complicating matters, to all those living in the area, was that Miles Hanley was viewed as one of Mac Shepard's closest friends. But secretly, Miles wanted nothing more than to see Mac Shepard – one way or another – lose his ranch.

It seemed, however, as far as the law was concerned, Mac Shepard had clean gotten away with the theft of the cattle. The injustice of the situation infuriated Miles, and he was going to make it his personal mission to make the cattle thief pay for his sins. It was bad enough that the sorry son-of-a-bitch stole cattle from honest men, but what upset Miles more was that the money Mac gained through the thefts allowed him to hang on to his ranch.

Miles had been lusting over that patch of fertile land for years and had done whatever he could to ensure Mac would lose it. Now it looked like that wasn't going to happen any time soon and Miles was growing impatient. From now on he would keep a close eye on Mac and do whatever he could to make sure Shepard lost everything he owned.

The following day, intent on his mission, Miles went into town early and sent off a telegram to the railroad's stationmaster trying to get information on the movement of trains the night before. No freight cars were scheduled to be in the area and all were accounted for, so that proved a frustrating dead end.

Miles had just finished attending to a couple of errands and was heading for his horse. As he stepped into the dusty street he met Sheriff Mason coming in the opposite direction. 'Good morning, Miles,' greeted the sheriff. 'What brings you into town so bright and early?'

'I'm doing your work,' Miles replied tersely.

The sheriff was a little confused at the statement and at Miles' disposition. Keeping his tone civil, he addressed the man. 'I'm not sure I understand what you're talking about, Miles.'

Miles was in no mood for idle chatter. 'You know

as well as I do Mac Shepard is dealing in stolen cattle. If you had bothered to ride out past his place last night you would have seen Mac and his son, Jason, paying off two other men. You would have smelled the cow shit, and you would have heard the damned train.'

The sheriff wasn't about to let Miles Hanley or anyone else tell him how to do his job. 'Miles, did you see any cattle?' he asked.

'No,' Miles snapped.

The lawman continued his questioning. 'Did you see a train?'

'No, but I heard it,' Miles retorted, his tone still combative.

'Hearing it doesn't mean a thing,' the sheriff countered. 'You know as well as I do the sound of a train can carry for miles on a cold night with no wind. And that's exactly the way it was last night.'

Miles was like a dog sucking the marrow from a dry bone. 'Well, what about me seeing Mac and his son paying off the two strangers?' When he saw the look of disbelief on the lawman's face, he continued. 'He told me he was paying off a ransom for Jason, but I know better than that.' He threw up his hands in frustration. 'Dammit, Mason, you and your deputies should have been there with me! The whole situation stinks like the shit I found them standing in, and you know it.'

Sheriff Mason had no desire to continue the conversation, so he shut Miles down. 'Miles, you have nothing. You didn't see one cow, you didn't see one train. Mac gave you a reason for the exchange of money. If Mac wants to report the incident, he's welcome to do so. If not, there's nothing I can do. You have no proof and that's what I need to go with, proof. Without it, we have nothing. So unless you have some solid evidence, I don't want to hear another word about it.'

Miles was clearly upset. His railroad inquiries had yielded nothing and now his conversation with Sheriff Mason had gone nowhere. He clenched his jaws and pushed pass the sheriff, only to change his mind and turn back to confront the man again, face red with anger; the big blue veins around the temples of his weather-beaten face were beginning to bulge. He jabbed his finger sharply in the air toward the sheriff as he resumed his rant. 'You know as well as I do Mac Shepard is rustling cattle. I smelled the shit, I heard the train and I caught him paying off the men who delivered them. I don't need any more evidence than that. If you're not going to do anything about it, I will, and that's a fact.' With that, Miles swiftly turned his back on the lawman and stalked away.

Sheriff Mason quickly called out. 'Miles Hanley, if you do anything illegal, you'll be the one behind bars. You keep that in mind!'

Ignoring the sheriff's warning, Miles kept on walking.

The last thing Sheriff Mason needed was to have Miles Hanley on the warpath. He knew Miles to be an honest man; but he also knew Miles could be ruthless when it came to business. As a lawman, he had heard stories of how Hanley had ended up with the XO. Stealing cattle might not sit well with the man, but acquiring land in a less than upright fashion was apparently a different story. So now he not only needed to keep an eye on Mac Shepard – who was certainly no innocent – he also needed to make sure Miles didn't go and do something stupid on him.

Andrew Crocker was a man of the cloth. His bones were old and frail, but his mind was still clear and his hearing still as sharp as the pocketknife he used for whittling. He was sitting in a chair on the boardwalk, knife in hand, as he did most days. Neither Miles nor Sheriff Mason paid attention to Andrew as they argued. But Andrew took in every word. He had lived in Fort Scott longer than Miles, Mac or Sheriff Joe Mason.

There was a time not too long ago when he preached the Sunday sermon, but he had given that position up to a younger man. His preaching days were over and his Bible had gone unopened for quite a spell. The townsfolk, including Mac, Miles and Joe, had given their 'confessions' to Andrew on numerous occasions.

He not only knew dark things about most of the people who lived in Fort Scott, he knew dark things about each of these three men. Things that would put their mothers to shame. Thieves each one of them in their own right.

Andrew could have easily ignored what he had just heard, but that wasn't his way. He didn't think much of Miles. His sin of choice was power, and he acquired it through the ownership of land. He bought it when he had to. He took it if he could. It didn't matter to Miles how much sweat the owner had poured into the land. If he could add it to his already vast holdings, he wanted it.

As for Mac, he was a thief and a man who had a blatant disregard for the rules and regulations that had been set in place by others. He played by his own, and didn't concern himself with how it affected those he was close to. Mac thought the world revolved around him. In a way, Andrew admired Mac's independence, but he loathed his lack of concern for others. He was surprised when his sister and his son came to stay with him. He thought just maybe Mac had matured, maybe even changed his ways, but what he heard this morning proved him wrong.

11

And Sheriff Joe Mason. He was law-abiding all right, but he was slothful and inefficient in the way he handled situations that were more involved and took some legwork. He would rather handle the simple tasks of his job like throwing drunks in jail. It took much less effort than trying to solve a cattle-rustling crime. Joe would have been better off if he had stayed a deputy, but pride and ego both have a way of creeping up on a man, and the offer of being the town's sheriff fed both.

Andrew was keenly observant of the goings-on around him. His mind was filled with the dark secrets and inside information of the people of Fort Scott. It was a heavy weight and an unwanted burden he now carried from his past profession. Just the same, if he ever needed to use it for good or for God, he most surely would.

Several days after the discussion between Miles and Sheriff Mason, a blank white envelope mysteriously showed up on Mac's doorstep. He unfolded it to find a note.

It read . . . *And they covet fields, and houses, and cattle and take them away: so they oppress a man and his house, even a man and his heritage. Therefore thus saith the Lord; Behold, against this family do I devise an evil, from which ye shall not remove your neck.*

It was signed, Micah.

The note took Mac by surprise. *Who would have put*

this note at his door? He thought, *Who knew of his past dealings? And just who the hell was Micah?*

There were only a few people involved with the deal he had made for the cattle. Someone could have slipped and said something to someone, or maybe Miles had left the note? If that was the case, what was he after? Did he want to see him swing or was this some sort of blackmail? At this point, Mac was sure about one thing only, he knew he didn't want to go to prison, or hang. He kept the note to himself. Jason and Sarah didn't need to be concerned with it.

Mac kept a low profile through the winter months. His mind worked overtime trying to figure it all out. He thought on how best to handle any accusations that might surface. If he was found out, he would be locked up or swinging from the end of a rope for sure. It was that last line of the note that played in his head the most. '. . . *I devise an evil, from which ye shall not remove your neck.*' The thought of swinging from a rope was beginning to unnerve him.

The business of the spring calving season helped to remove the burden of a guilty conscience from his mind. That didn't change the fact that elsewhere and ever so slowly, the wheels of almighty justice were in motion.

Calving season had ended and the cows had been turned out. Now with a little breathing room, Mac's son, Jason, began to grow restless. It was time to move on. He let Mac know of his intentions over breakfast one morning. Mac tried to talk him out of it, but Jason's stubborn side was having none of it. He was beginning to understand his true nature and for the time being it was not one that allowed him to sit still for any length of time. Maybe that would change over time, but for now, it was what it was.

Anxious to see more of the world he had only heard about, he headed west out of Fort Scott with all of his worldly possessions, which consisted of little more than a good horse, a change of clothes, a bedroll, and three hundred dollars in his front pocket. He was off to see what he might find beyond the town of Fort Scott and beyond the far horizon.

Jason was truly the adventurous type and had no intention of heading straight out of Kansas without making a stop in Wichita and possibly Dodge City. Even though he was raised near Wichita, he was never allowed to go into town. *Too dangerous, not for young boys* and *you're needed here at home,* were the usual excuses given by the couple who had raised him. Now that he was on his own, he had every intention of experiencing the places he had only heard about. From there he would make his decision either to head further west or to follow the Chisholm down into Texas.

*

14

As Jason approached Wichita, he considered taking a slight detour and riding out to the place where he was raised, but a second thought showed better judgement and he decided against it. No sense in reliving a bitter past that was better left dead and buried along with the man that created the bitterness to begin with. Sarah, Jason's stepmother, had put the place up for sale after the death of her husband. It now had new owners and a new lease on life, just as he did. His decision to head straight for town seemed to be the better choice.

Along the trail between Fort Scott and Wichita, Jason had seen few riders and fewer wagons, but the closer he got to town, the more camps he passed at its outskirts. An old, hastily painted sign hung from a short pole that had been planted beside the road. The sign read 'Everything Goes in Wichita'. To the south, a thick cloud of dust billowed high in the afternoon sky. It hung over the holding pens where many of the longhorns coming up from Texas could be seen. Out of curiosity, Jason headed toward the dust, where the smell of cow dung and dirt hung heavy in the air. Jason was amazed at the sights and sounds of so much activity, but this was nothing more than a prelude to the human activity he would soon find when he headed deeper into the heart of Wichita.

After spending a couple of hours soaking in all the

commotion of the stockyards, Jason decided he needed to do another type of soaking to rid himself of the layer of trail dust he had picked up over the past few days. A hot bath and something to eat were heavy on his mind and he planned to make it his next order of business, so he rode on across the railroad tracks and toward the town square. He was surprised by the sheer number of people that were busying themselves along the boardwalk and the street. *There don't seem to be enough buildings to hold so many people, which explains the large number of camps outside of town,* he thought to himself.

As he worked his way through the bustle he kept an eye out for a place to stable his horse. He soon found what he was looking for and made the necessary arrangements. With his saddlebags draped over his shoulder, he wandered the town, eagerly taking in all the sights he had heard so much about as he looked for a place to take a bath. Several new buildings were in various stages of completion. A half-dozen saloons and almost as many brothels lined the main street. Horses and wagons were coming and going, busily involved in the commerce of the day. The sounds of hammers, horses and pianos filled the air. This was indeed a boomtown and Jason had never seen the likes of it before now.

As he meandered about, he spied a small painted

sign nailed to the side of a building, offering 'Hot Bath 25¢'. Under that was an arrow pointing to the left. Jason made the turn and headed straight for the door. He stepped into the building and up to the front counter where he was met by the proprietor, an older, portly man, clean-shaven and smartly dressed. He wore a bowler hat and smelled of an unknown fragrance that overpowered the room.

'How do you do, young man! Welcome to the Wichita Bath and Brothel. Step lively, girls,' summoned the man behind the counter as he clapped his hands and called for several young ladies to move to the front of the room.

The girls stepped out from behind a curtain at the back of the room and moved closer to Jason. The portly man removed his hat and waved it about as he began his well-rehearsed speech. 'We offer the cleanest ladies in all of Wichita, young man. A hot bath is only twenty-five cents, but for a mere two dollars more, one of these fine young ladies will not only wash your hair and scrub your back, they will most certainly bedazzle and entertain you after you're clean and dry. What do you say to *that*, young man? Are you looking for nothing more than a plain and simple bath, or would you rather enjoy a most fulfilling and entertaining bathing experience?'

The women were seductive and scantily dressed, to the point of showing their legs well above the knee.

Jason had just wanted a bath, but now he didn't know what to think. It was indeed a temptation of the kind he had only dreamed about, but never before encountered.

'Well, what will it be, young man?' asked the proprietor. 'Speak up or I'll have to charge you for looking.'

Jason was spellbound and a bit hesitant about making such a major decision, but he finally got the words out of his mouth. 'I, I guess, what the heck. I'll take the two-dollar bath.'

'Excellent choice, young man,' the proprietor quickly replied. 'Your hot bath is being drawn as we speak. You may choose the woman of your dreams, but first, that will be two dollars and twenty five cents.'

Jason paid the man and picked for himself a lovely young woman with long black hair and big breasts. The proprietor hadn't lied. He was given the bathing experience of his life and then some. He walked out of the building leaving behind a tub full of dirty water and his virginity. It would certainly be the one bath he would never forget.

It was late in the day and the noonday sun had given way to the twilight sky. Jason rented a room at one of several boarding houses in town and stowed his gear. As he stepped out for the evening, there was a definite newfound vigor to his step and a gleam in his eye that had never been there before. He felt charmed, as if 'Lady Luck' was on his side and all he touched would turn to gold. There was a saloon not far down the street called the Customs House; Jason decided to see if he could sit in on a game of cards for the evening.

The Customs House wasn't as big as he anticipated, and it was crowded. Jason searched the room for an opening at one of several card games in progress, but none were available. There was also no room at the bar other than an open spot where he could order a drink. After buying a beer he sat down at a small round table with an empty chair. Two men were sharing a bottle of whiskey. Jason took a friendly tone and struck up a conversation with them. One of the men, a middle-aged fellow with salt-and-pepper hair and a mustache to match, seemed friendly enough. He introduced himself as Cal Collins. The other, an older man whose sun-baked, leathered face was cut deep with the wrinkles of a hard life and tempered with age, was less than enthusiastic about conversing with Jason and let him know it. 'If you don't mind, son, we're having a private conversation here.'

Jason didn't have to be told twice. 'Didn't mean to intrude,' he replied. As he got up to leave the table, Cal motioned for him to sit back down, then turned to his partner.

'Hey, don't worry about it, Hap. A private conversation ain't gonna happen in here. We'll talk about this later.'

Hap replied with an urgent tone. 'I can't wait for later, Cal. I need an answer now. The longer we wait, the further away he gets.'

'I don't have an answer for you right now, Hap,' replied Cal.

Hap was obviously unhappy with the shortness of Cal's reply. 'Then I'll take that as a no. I'll do this on my own.'

'He's deadly, Hap,' replied Cal. The tone of his voice showed a real sense of concern. 'It'll be a fool's errand if you do.'

'I'll take my chances,' Hap replied angrily as he downed his whiskey and slammed the glass on the table. 'Thanks for the drink.'

He got up and headed in the general direction of the faro table before disappearing into the crowd.

Jason was apologetic. 'I didn't mean to interrupt a business meeting.'

'Don't worry about it,' replied Cal. 'That man has no patience. He could get us both killed.'

'How's that?' asked Jason.

'He wants my help in catching a man by the name of Stewart Clayton. Ever heard of him?'

'No, can't say that I have.'

Cal leaned in toward Jason. 'Stewart Clayton is an

outlaw of the worst kind. A cold-blooded killer. Wears his hair long, usually braided, like a woman . . . or maybe an Indian. He's called the 'Chisholm Bandit' cuz he likes to rob cattle drovers as they head back home from a long cattle drive. They got money in their pocket and he knows it. Not that long ago a couple of Texas boys took offense to him tryin' to rob 'em. They got into a shootin' match over it. One of the boys died, and the other took a bullet in the arm, and as for Stewart Clayton, he got away with all their money and not much more than a scratch. He may not know it yet, but he had the door slammed shut on his outlaw career last week when he shot himself a woman. He was in the process of robbing the noon stage just outside of town. I guess she had something he wanted and she wasn't about to give it up. Her big mistake was to sass him. He called her a bitch and I guess it must have been a natural reaction on her part, but nonetheless, she slapped him for it. Stewart didn't take kindly to it. Without so much as a second's hesitation, he shot her dead and took it off her body. Rumor has it she was the wife of some rich banker type with political connections. That was enough to put a nice bounty on his head.'

'What was he after?' asked Jason inquisitively.

'Some piece of jewelry, I hear; a brooch or a locket maybe. Whatever it was, it caught his eye and he wanted it.' replied Cal. 'Anyhow, Hap's been trailing him. Says he knows where he's heading, but he needs my help to flush him out once he catches up to him. I ain't that excited about working with the man. I did a couple years back and ended up with a bullet in my arm because he couldn't sit tight long enough to do the job right. It's like I said, the man has no patience.'

'How much is the bounty?' inquired Jason.

'Well, that depends on the day.' replied Cal. 'The woman's husband opened an account at the bank. I guess you could call it a "Bounty Account" of sorts, and he put a thousand dollars into it. Wealthy friends and a few sympathetic town folk have been adding to it almost daily. Last I heard it was close to two thousand dollars. But there's a catch. The husband wants Stewart Clayton brought back alive so he can have the pleasure of watching him hang.'

Jason's interest was growing by the minute. 'Two thousand dollars is a lot of money. If you don't want any of it, maybe I'll go find Hap and see if I can talk my way into helping him out.'

Cal's demeanor quickly changed from casual to serious. His kindly smile left his face as he once again leaned in close and looked Jason square in the eye. 'Have you ever tracked a man with a bounty on his head?' he questioned.

'No, I haven't,' replied Jason cautiously.

'Well, let me tell you a thing or two, young man,

I've seen my share of 'em, and they're as ruthless as can be. Ain't nothin' meaner than a wanted man backed into a corner. Hap, he's got some experience behind him, no doubt about it. If he'd just learn to have a bit of patience, he'd be just fine. Thing is, I can't see him hookin' up with an inexperienced kid. Why, he might as well sign his own death warrant. No offense, son, but you're still wet behind the ears. You need to get yourself some life experience behind the business end of a gun before you take on huntin' outlaws for a livin'. Hap and I were both deputies for a spell. In fact, I was a sheriff for a couple of years. It's a good way to learn how to handle men like Stewart Clayton. Believe me, it ain't like huntin' jack rabbits.'

Cal picked up his bottle of whiskey and poured himself another shot. 'Care for a drink, young man?'

'No thanks,' replied Jason as he grabbed his beer and got up from the table. 'I think I'll see if I can find Hap.'

Cal downed his drink and slammed the palm of his hand down on to the table. The look he gave Jason firmly revealed his displeasure at the comment. 'Boy, you ain't heard a single word I said, now have you? I'm tellin' you, Hap would be a fool to have anything to do with you.'

'I think I'll find that out for myself, if you don't mind,' replied Jason.

Cal poured another drink as Jason walked off.

'You're a stubborn little bastard,' he called out as he downed the shot.

Jason headed toward the faro table as he scouted the crowded room looking for Hap. He soon found him standing by the bar waiting for an opening at one of several poker tables. Jason stepped up beside him. Hap, who was a head taller, kept his eye on the table he wanted to sit at, but had noticed Jason step up beside him. 'You following me, boy?'

'The name is Jason, and that would be a yes. I hear you're after Stewart Clayton?'

Hap was surprised to hear that, and gave up his focus on the table. He turned toward Jason with a sense of curiosity. 'How the hell do you know that?'

'Cal told me,' he replied.

'Cal needs to learn to keep his trap shut, and why the hell is Stewart Clayton any concern to you? Do you even know the man?'

'No,' replied Jason. 'But I'd like to help you catch him.'

'Help me catch him?' Hap let out a laugh. 'You've got to be joking. I'll bet you're not more than a year or two off your mammy's pap. Why in hell would I even consider taking you up on that? It's a sure way to get myself killed. I know that for a fact.'

'Well I'm not going to press it,' answered Jason.

'That would be a damn good decision,' replied Hap.

Jason went on. 'I just figured since Cal wasn't interested, you might be looking for someone to give you a hand. I've got more under my hat than you give me credit for, and *I* know *that* for a fact.'

'Well then, you should want to keep it there, kid. You go chasing after bad men like Stewart Clayton, you'd most likely get your brains blown out. I have to admit, I like your spunk, but the fact is, Cal and I have worked together in the past and we've found ourselves in some pretty tight situations. I know I can trust him to have my back. Can't say that about you.' Hap turned his attention back to the poker table.

Jason stood next to Hap and concentrated on the same table. 'Do you see what I'm seeing?' asked Jason.

'What's that?' replied Hap.

'If you're planning on sitting in on that table there,' he motioned to the one close to the window, 'Be sure the dandy in the bowler is the one to leave the opening.'

'And why should I do that?' replied Hap inquiringly.

'Because he's cheating.'

Hap focused his attention on the dandy. 'How do you know that?'

'Keep an eye on him the next time he shuffles. He's stacking the deck, I'm sure of it.'

Hap watched as the dandy shuffled the deck, then

remarked, 'I think you're seeing things kid. It looked legit to me.'

Hap no sooner got the words out of his mouth when the young man sitting across from the dandy stood up in a huff and pointed an accusing finger straight at him. 'You're cheatin'. You're stackin' the deck, I saw it.'

Before the dandy had a chance to rebut the accusation, one of the two deputies assigned to the floor stepped forward. 'What's the problem here, mister?'

The accuser restated his accusation. 'He's cheatin'. I saw it.'

Of course the dandy vehemently denied it. At that point the deputy called the game over. All four men had to get up and leave the table while another four sat down for a new game. Hap was one of the four. Hap looked up at Jason. 'Kid, you got a good eye, I'll give you that much.'

The accuser was still visibly upset from the whole situation and probably a little bit drunk as well. He began to verbally abuse one of the women working the room. She was standing next to Jason. He minded his own business until the young man slapped the woman with the back of his hand. Jason immediately flashed back to his stepfather, Jim and how he would beat him and his wife, Sarah. Without thinking twice, Jason stepped in between the two of them.

'Get the hell out of my way, you little red-headed runt, or I'll drop you right here and now,' shouted the accuser.

The men standing in the vicinity stopped what they were doing to assess the situation. Jason was on the spot. He knew how to defend himself. He'd had years of practice blocking Jim's blows, and the fights he had gotten into at school taught him how to throw a mean punch.

'I said . . . get the hell out of my way,' bellowed the accuser one more time.

One of the deputies stood nearby, but wasn't about to break something up that hadn't really started yet. Jason didn't waste any more time staring the man down. He sucker-punched him with a quick right hook to the side of the head and the accuser went down, hitting the floor like a sack of spuds. He was out cold. Jason walked toward the door and since there was no fight to break up, the deputy let him go.

As Jason stepped out into the street a voice called him from behind. 'Young man, excuse me, young man.'

Jason turned to see a thin middle-aged man wearing a top hat and tails. A thin mustache covered his upper lip. He held a lit cigar in his left hand as he held out his right in a friendly gesture.

'Good evening, young sir. My name is Melvin, Melvin D. Winkel,' he continued.

'That's one hell of a name,' replied Jason.

'Yes, yes it is, thank you,' replied Melvin. He continued, 'I couldn't help but see what just transpired within this establishment. I haven't seen such a powerful right hook in quite some time, and I don't believe I've ever seen one from such a young man as yourself. May I inquire as to your nationality? If my guess is correct, I would venture to say that the redness of your hair marks you as Irish; would I be mistaken?'

'My mother was Irish,' replied Jason hesitantly. 'Why do you care?'

Melvin continued. 'I care because the Irish are known as being bullheaded and good scrappers.'

'Like I said,' replied Jason, 'Why do you care?'

'I care, young man, because your Irish background and your red hair can make you a lot of money, if you'll be so kind as to hear me out.'

Jason was interested. 'Go on, I'm listening.'

'Here's my card.' Melvin handed Jason his business card. Jason glanced down at the card and read out loud 'Melvin D Winkel, Boxing Promoter.'

'That's correct, young man. I promote honest and fair boxing exhibitions for the enjoyment of those who care to watch. I have established an arena just outside of town. A large tent in which I charge two bits to each patron who enters. I also take bets on the side. If you win, we split the take fifty-fifty. I believe you can win most any man willing to go up against you.'

'You saw me throw one punch,' replied Jason. 'So what makes you think I can win most any man?'

'Because the man you so coldly knocked out was one of my best fighters.'

'I sucker-punched him. He wasn't even expecting it,' answered Jason.

'Well then, a rematch is in order, would you not agree?' inquired Melvin.

'No, I would not agree,' replied Jason, shortly. 'Goodnight.'

Jason walked off, leaving Melvin standing in the street.

'You have my card if you should change your mind,' he called out.

Without turning around, Jason dropped the card into the street and kept walking. Melvin walked over and retrieved it. Little bastard, he thought, *I need him.*

Jason continued on to his room. He was tired and decided to call it a day.

CHAPTER 2

HARD WAY OUT

It was early the following morning and Jason was up before the sun; the cloudless night had been the harbinger of a biting cold morning. Having decided it was time to move on, Jason wasn't about to lose a minute of daylight. He needed to pick up a few supplies on the way out of town; the general store was close by and he hoped it would be open early. Jason was feeling good about the day, as he had made his decision and his direction would be south to Texas. There were plenty of men heading that way. Most were on their way home after delivering their cattle. His thought was that it would be safer if he hooked up with several others. After what Cal had told him and the rumors he had been hearing that there were desperados in the open country waiting to rob any drover who took it upon himself to travel solo, or even with several others in a small group, he didn't want to take any chances.

He reached the store and was thankful to find it open. As he walked in he was met by a very cheerful proprietor and a warm stove. He stepped up to it and warmed his hands.

'Good morning, young man. It's a bit cold out there today, isn't it? How may I help you?' the merchant asked.

'I need a few supplies,' Jason replied.

'Let me guess,' ventured the proprietor. 'You just delivered your cattle and now you're ready to head back to Texas. Am I right?'

'Close enough,' replied Jason as he continued to warm his hands.

'I have men coming in here every day searching for the same things before they head out. I've taken the liberty of assembling an assortment of the most necessary supplies into one package. Take a look at this list if you like.' The proprietor handed Jason a slip of paper with a list of supplies on it.

'If you're agreeable to it,' continued the proprietor, 'I'll let you have the whole lot for my special price of only five dollars. What do you say?'

Jason looked over the list and gave it short consideration. He agreed it was a fair price. Reaching into his front pocket he pulled out his money and paid the man. The proprietor handed him one of several cloth sacks filled with his supplies. As he headed for the door he stopped short and asked the proprietor, 'Is there a telegraph office in town? I need to send a message to Fort Scott.'

'Yes, there is, it's just down the street to your right,' he thoughtfully replied. 'Do you have kin in Fort Scott?'

'I do,' replied Jason.

'I have a brother who lives in Fort Scott. Perhaps you know of him?' inquired the proprietor. 'He owns the Fort Scott Mercantile, His name is Ira.'

Surprised, Jason almost dropped his supplies when he heard the name. 'Ira, yes, I know Ira,' he replied calmly. 'In fact, the next time you see him, tell him the red-haired kid wants to know how his head is. He'll understand.'

'His head? OK, I'll do that,' replied the puzzled proprietor.

As Jason moved toward the door he walked past a glass display case that held a couple of pistols. A mischievous grin crossed his face as he seriously thought about spitting on it as he had done at Ira's mercantile, but he passed it by, thinking better of it.

Jason took the supplies back to his room and tossed them on the bed. Then he immediately headed off to the telegraph office.

As he headed happily down the boardwalk his way was suddenly blocked by the man he had knocked out the night before. Melvin stood off in the background, grinning. Jason tensed up, not knowing what to expect from the man. He was in a good mood and really didn't want this confrontation.

'You sucker-punched me last night,' the man stated angrily. 'I don't take kindly to that.'

'You shouldn't have been slapping around a woman. I don't take kindly to *that*. As far as I'm concerned, you got what you deserved.' Jason tried to end the conversation by walking around the man, but a quick sidestep prevented it.

Melvin calmly puffed on one of his thin cigars as he watched the carefully calculated altercation.

'Like I said, kid, I don't take kindly to being sucker-punched. I want a fair fight. We can do it now or we can do it . . . .'

It was at this point Melvin stepped up and cut the man off in mid-sentence. 'Now listen here, son. You can have it out with Luther here and now, or you can do it tonight. Here and now will get you nothing, but if you choose tonight, I'll pay you fifty dollars.'

'What happened to the fifty-fifty deal you offered me yesterday?' Jason retorted.

'That was yesterday, young man. Today it's fifty dollars, or as I stated, nothing if you choose to do it now.'

Jason could see he was in a no-win situation. One way or another he was going to have to fight Luther. Melvin had seen to that. 'You're an underhanded son-of-a-bitch, Melvin.'

Yes, yes I am,' Melvin replied snidely. His smile was a good indication that he liked the title.

'How much are you paying Luther?' Jason inquired.

'The same,' Melvin replied.

Jason considered it thoughtfully before he replied. 'OK, I'll do it, but under one condition.'

Melvin was extremely pleased to hear Jason's change of heart. 'And what might that be?' he hastily inquired.

Jason replied forcefully. 'The condition is that I'll only fight if the winner gets one hundred and the loser gets nothing. Take it or leave it.'

Luther was confident and seemed pleased with the condition as he turned an eye toward Melvin. Melvin readily agreed. It really didn't matter to him. The fight was lined up and he would make money from it no matter how things turned out.

Jason was unhappy with this turn of events. He was packed and ready to leave, but now it would have to wait until tomorrow. Another hundred dollars in his pocket would be a welcome consolation, or so he thought.

Melvin spoke up. 'Be at the tent on the north edge

of town at seven o'clock tonight.'

'Don't back out on me,' added Luther. 'I'm gonna beat your ass bloody.' He stepped aside and let Jason pass.

The altercation had flustered Jason so much he almost forgot he was heading to the telegraph office. He quickly put it behind him and continued on.

He got to the office just as Hap was stepping out. 'Good morning, Hap,' greeted Jason with a smile. 'I thought you might be out of town by now?'

'Not yet,' he replied as he sat himself down in an empty chair by the door. He pulled out a match and struck it against his boot, then used it to light the quirly he held in the corner of his mouth. 'Cal is still on the fence about helping me on this one. I may have to go it alone.'

'My offer still stands to go with you,' offered Jason.

'Like I said last night, I need an experienced man with me, not some greenhorn kid. I don't want either one of us getting killed, and believe me, Stewart Clayton would be just the man to do it. Cal will come around. I only hope he does it sooner than later.'

'Maybe he's waiting for the reward money to grow,' offered Jason.

'No, he's just getting soft on me. I guess it's time to go put a burr under his blanket.' Hap took one last drag and flicked the smoke into the road, stood up and wandered off to have another talk with Cal.

Jason shrugged, and crossed the threshold into the telegraph office.

'Good morning, young man,' greeted the woman behind the counter as Jason stepped up to it. 'What can I do for you today?'

Behind the counter, Jason could see a middle-aged man writing as the ticker frantically clicked off its message. 'I never will understand how all that clicking can be saying something understandable,' remarked Jason.

'It's one of the miracles of our modern age,' the woman replied as she stood ready with pencil in hand. 'Where would you like to send your message?' she inquired.

'I'd like to send it to Fort Scott, to a Ms. Sarah McKinney.'

'And what would you like it to say?' she asked.

'Say, I'm fine, sorry I won't make your wedding. Heading to Texas. I'll be back, I promise, Jason.'

'That's it?' she questioned.

'Yep, that's it,' replied Jason.

'That'll be thirty cents, please.'

Jason paid the woman and walked out of the office. He sat down in the empty chair by the door. He had nothing to do until later that evening. The cold morning air was beginning to lose its edge and the sun radiating off the side of the building felt good. He was enjoying the moment when Hap and

Cal rode by. They reined in their horses when they spied Jason lounging on the porch of the telegraph office.

'Is it true you're going to fight Luther tonight?' asked Hap.

Jason got up from the chair and stepped to the edge of the boardwalk. With his hands in his pockets he leaned up against a post. 'I guess that's the plan,' replied Jason. 'Don't really want to, but he didn't leave me much choice.'

'I've seen him fight. He has a mean left jab. You'd do well to steer clear of it if you can,' advised Hap.

'Thanks for the advice, Hap. I appreciate it. On Stewart Clayton's trail, are you?' questioned Jason.

'Yep, we've come to terms,' Cal interjected. 'Hap got word this morning that he was seen heading toward Fort Scott. We've got some hard ridin' to do if we expect to catch up to him any time soon. You take care of yourself now. Maybe we'll meet up again someday. Oh, one more word of advice. If you win, get out of town before that promoter signs you up for another. He has a silver tongue, that one.'

They turned their horses and galloped toward the edge of town.

Seven o'clock came way too soon. Jason showed up at the tent to find Melvin impatiently waiting at the flap with his pocket watch in hand. 'It's about time,' he pointed to his watch for emphasis. 'I thought you might have skipped town on me. I have fifty betting men in here just itching to see someone get the tar beat out of them. Don't let me down and win this fight now. I'll make more if you lose, get my drift?'

'I get your drift,' replied Jason as he faced Melvin. 'I don't trust you to pay me if I win so I want my hundred dollars now.'

Melvin laughed in Jason's face. 'Do you take me for a fool, boy? I'll pay you *if* you win, and I hope to hell you don't.'

'You'll pay me now or I don't go in,' insisted Jason. 'If Luther wins, you can take your money back easily enough. Remember, you have fifty betting men in there. It would be a shame to disappoint them, now wouldn't it?'

Melvin considered the situation before relenting. 'You're a real son-of-a-bitch, you know that?'

'Takes one to know one,' replied Jason.

Melvin scoffed at the comment as he counted out one hundred dollars and handed it to Jason. Jason took the money and jammed it deep into his front pocket, then walked into the tent.

Melvin walked behind him with his hands on his shoulders as he steered him through the crowd of anxious men, and a few women as well. The tent was hot and the air hung heavy with a thick cloud of tobacco smoke. Luther was already in the ring. For some reason, Jason thought, the man looked a lot bigger than he had when they were together in the street.

Once in the ring, Jason removed his hat and shirt. He could hear the crowd remarking about his red hair and well-trimmed upper body. There were a few side bets taking place after they got a good look at him.

Melvin stepped into the ring and motioned to the crowd to quiet down so he could speak. Once he had their attention he introduced the two fighters and reminded them this was a gentleman's fight. No kicking, biting or spitting on the opponent. They would fight until one man could no longer get up.

Once the rules were stated and they both agreed, he let the two have at it.

Luther wanted retribution and he came out swinging. Jason, having warded off many a blow from his abusive stepfather, easily defended himself. A minute into the fight the crowd was growing restless. Luther was throwing all the punches and Jason had yet to throw one.

Melvin stood next to Jason and began to yell, 'Come on boy, mix it up. The crowd is against you.'

Jason could care less about the crowd. He took a step back while Luther caught his breath. Luther came back at him with a couple of those left jabs Hap had warned him about. In an instant, something deep inside Jason snapped. He no longer saw Luther throwing punches, he saw his stepfather, Jim. And the urge to kill overtook him. Jason let loose with several body blows that took Luther by surprise and backed him up several feet. When Luther came back at him with a strong left, Jason saw his opening. He moved his head back out of reach and when Luther's hand went past his face Jason let loose with a devastating right hook to the side of Luther's head. It was placed so well, you could hear the jawbone shatter above the din of the crowd. Once again, Jason's right hand had taken Luther down and put him out cold.

The roar of the crowd could be heard all the way into town. Melvin was indeed not happy with the results and he let Jason know it. But even before Jason had a chance to pick up his shirt and hat, Melvin was trying to sign him up to a contract. Jason wanted no part of it. He didn't mind a good fight, especially when it paid well, but he didn't want to make a living out of it.

Jason went back to town and walked into the Customs House for a cold beer. As he entered the room, several of the men who had been at the fight cheered him and thanked him for winning their bets for them. They even paid for his beer. As he stood at the bar the girl who he had protected the previous night from the hand of Luther came up beside him and held out twenty-five dollars.

'What's this?' he asked.

'I took bets that you would win, and you did. This is to show my appreciation for what you did for me the other night.'

Jason looked at her closely. She was pretty. Older than him, probably in her twenties. He took her hand and folded her long fingers back around the money. 'It's a nice gesture ma'am,' he replied, 'but you won it. I think you should keep it.'

She smiled, put the money in a safe pocket on her dress, then without a word, she took Jason by the hand and led him up the stairs.

The following morning Jason woke up in his own bed. Even though he had wanted to be out of town by now, yesterday had proved itself to be quite profitable in more ways than one. Now he was more serious than ever about heading south toward Texas. He already had his supplies. All he needed to do was hook up with a few other men who were heading south after delivering their cattle. Right now, breakfast was on his mind. He had eaten light yesterday and now he was hungry. There was a small café across the street called the Blue Bell. It looked like a nice place, so he thought he'd give it a try.

As soon as Jason stepped through the door of the Blue Bell, he was cheerfully greeted by a middle-aged man who was busily cooking over the stove. He raised his spatula in greeting as he turned the hotcakes in front of him. 'Good morning, sir. Have a seat. My wife will be with you shortly. She had to step out back for a minute. Coffee runs right through the woman.'

Jason grinned and acknowledged the gesture with one of his own in return. The place was bright and cheery. Each table was covered with a blue-checkered cloth and had a small vase of fresh flowers on it. Several tables had customers. What they were eating looked good and the smell coming from the cooking area was confirmation enough that it would taste as good as it looked.

Jason stepped over to the counter to sit, just as the cook's wife walked in from out back. 'Good morning, young man,' she greeted as she dried her wet hands on the apron she had just put on. She poured him a generous cup of hot coffee without so much as asking if he wanted it.

'Coffee's on the house,' she stated as she laid a menu on the counter. 'What can I get you?'

Jason didn't need the menu. He knew exactly what he wanted. 'Hotcakes, a couple eggs and some bacon,' he replied. 'And thanks for the coffee.'

'You're welcome. Did you get that, dear?' she asked her husband at the stove close by.

He repeated the order. 'Hotcakes, eggs and bacon. Got it.'

Jason was enjoying a bit of small talk when Melvin

came through the door and sat down beside him. He rudely cut off the waitress in mid-sentence. 'Excuse me, ma'am, but I have some important business to discuss with this young man.'

The cook looked up from his work with a suspicious eye. He didn't like the tone or the rudeness to his wife, but he knew she could hold her own, so didn't make any moves toward Melvin.

The waitress let it go. It was just small talk.

Melvin pulled out a piece of paper and a pencil from his pocket and laid it on the counter in front of Jason. 'I happened to see you step in here, son, and I'm glad I did. This is your lucky day. I know you were not in a, shall we say "receptive" mood to talk business last night. I'm sure you've had plenty of time to reconsider your hasty reply. I've taken the liberty of drawing up a formal agreement that is sure to make you a wealthy man. All you need to do is sign your name here on the bottom. If you don't know how to write, any hen scratching will suffice.'

Jason had no desire to talk with Melvin and even less desire to fight for him. Without a word, he picked up the paper and tore it in half, grabbed up the pencil, broke off the tip and snapped it in two. He then shoved all the pieces back toward Melvin. The couple behind the counter were grinning almost to the point of laughter, but they contained themselves.

Melvin's eyes widened as he watched Jason. 'This is a big mistake, young man, a big mistake. We would have made a lot of money, you and I. Do you hear me, a lot of money!' Melvin got up and turned toward the door. He left as quickly as he had come in.

'What the hell was that all about?' asked the cook.

'That bastard. . . .' Jason caught himself. 'Sorry, ma'am. I didn't mean to curse in front of you. That scoundrel wanted to use me to make *himself* a lot of money. I may be young in age, but I'm no fool to the ways of cheats and scoundrels. Besides, I'm leaving this morning for Texas.'

The cook set a plate of hot food in front of Jason. 'The morning's running long. You better eat up.'

Jason took the cook's advice and did just that. The food was delicious.

As he ate, a couple of men came in and sat at the counter next to Jason. They looked a bit older than him and by their appearance he figured they were drovers that had recently come off the trail. The two men ordered breakfast and talked between themselves. Jason listened in and from what he gathered, these two men were about to leave town.

Jason lingered with his food as the two men ate heartily. When they had about finished he struck up a conversation with them.

'I couldn't help overhearing some of your

44

conversation. Are the two of you planning to head out of town today?'

'Yes, in fact we are,' replied one of the men.

'Where to?' inquired Jason.

'We're heading back to the Square D, close to Dallas, Texas. Why the questions?'

Jason could sense the tone of the conversation was beginning to become more guarded so he quickly introduced himself. 'I'm sorry for the questions. My name is Jason, Jason McKinney.' He extended his hand in friendship, which both drovers accepted.

Jason continued. 'I'm planning to leave town today myself and it just so happens I'm going your direction. I've heard the trail can be pretty dangerous.'

'How so?' inquired one of the drovers.

'In that there are robbers on the lookout for drovers heading south. They know they've just been paid and are looking for easy targets. I've heard it's better to travel with a few others,' Jason replied.

'We've heard that ourselves and were planning to hitch up with a couple others before we left town. You're welcome to come with us if you like. My name's Teddy and this here's Bret.' Teddy pointed to his partner and they all shook hands in agreement that they would head south together. They settled up their bill as they got up to leave.

'What outfit did you come up here with?' asked Bret.

'I'm from here,' replied Jason as he put on his hat. 'I'm looking to see some of this country. I thought I'd start with finding out where all these cows are coming from.'

Bret had to chuckle at that. 'Some of the boys who come up here want to stay, and you, you want to head to Texas. Well, there's plenty to see between here and there and we'll be happy to show it to you. Won't we, Teddy?'

'Every last mile of it,' replied Teddy. 'We have to grab the rest of our gear before we head out. It's at the livery.'

'Perfect,' replied Jason. 'My horse is there, but my gear is at the boarding house where I'm staying. I'll meet you at the livery in, say, thirty minutes?'

'We'll be there,' they both replied.

Jason headed for the boarding house to grab his gear. *Finally*, he thought. *I wasn't sure if I was going to make it out today or not.*

As Jason reached the livery Teddy and Bret were waiting, along with two other riders. 'Hey, Jason. Looks like we picked up two more. This here is Owen and the skinny one here is Pat. They're both part of our outfit. I guess they had a change of heart about staying on.'

Owen was a big man. Clean-shaven except for a

thick salt-and-pepper mustache. His eyes were very intense and looked like they could stare a hole right through a man. He touched the brim of his hat and gave a slight nod of his head. 'Pleased to meet you,' he stated.

Pat, on the other hand, was much smaller, almost petite in size, with a much lighter complexion. Jason thought he looked rather feminine in an odd sort of way. When Pat held out a hand in friendship and began to speak his thoughts were confirmed.

'How do you do there, Jason. My name is Patricia. Pat for short. I love the color of your hair.'

Jason accepted the handshake. Pat held his a bit longer than what would be considered normal. She gave him a wide smile as she slowly slipped her hand from his. Jason noticed her hair tucked under her hat. It was red.

'I think Pat here is more a boy than a girl,' teased Bret. 'I think her father would have rather had a boy. He raised her like one. He owns the cattle we delivered. I think that's the only reason she tagged along.'

'Hey, that's not fair! I held my own,' boasted Pat.

'Yes you did, and then some,' agreed Bret with a quick wink and a smile.

'We could sit here and gab all day, but we need to get going,' interjected Owen with an air of authority. Looking down at Jason, he remarked. 'Have you got a horse, or are you walking?'

'I have a horse,' replied Jason. 'Let me grab it.'

Jason went in, settled up his bill and saddled his horse. When he returned, they were off.

CHAPTER 3

BAD FEELINGS

Jason, Teddy, Owen, Bret and Pat rode out of Wichita and headed south. 'It took us two months to deliver our cattle and we're a thousand miles from home,' stated Owen. 'I don't know about the rest of you, but I don't plan on taking another two months to get back to the Square D, I'm setting a pace of at least forty miles a day. You all need to keep up.'

No one objected as they were all anxious to get back home, and Jason was looking forward to putting Kansas behind him.

The first week went by without a hitch. Everyone was in high spirits, joking and carrying on. Quite often a cloud of dust could be seen off in the distance as herds of Texas longhorns made their way north. No one in the group envied the men who pushed those cattle to market. As the days went by, the angst to get home was beginning to show on a couple of the boys. Owen continued to push the pace and they continued to make good time. Pat had taken a good-natured liking to Jason, and he had openly welcomed her friendship. They rode side by side most days, and in the evening stayed up later than the others, talking by the firelight.

Early one afternoon, during the second week of their journey, the sky began to darken quickly as billowing storm clouds began to gather. 'Storm's a comin',' shouted Owen. 'We need to find cover.'

'Let's try for that stand of trees over yonder,' suggested Teddy as he pointed off to their right. The sky was growing darker by the minute as they raced for the trees, the wind had ceased to blow and the air felt almost electric. They had all been through this before. Texas had its own storms and this one was no different. They were fortunate not to have run into one on their way to Wichita. It could have easily spooked the cattle into a stampede. The lightning alone could kill cattle, horses and men, and it could take days to gather what was left of the scattered herd. This storm looked nasty by any measure.

Jason had been through these storms as well and he knew that a bolt of lightning would be attracted to the highest point. Out in the open as they were, he wanted that to be his horse and not him. Thunder began to rumble and lightning flashed just in front of them. 'No time to run,' shouted Jason. 'Spread out, get off your horse and tie it to a bush. Keep away from your horse and crouch down low,' he continued.

Jason, Pat and Owen knew the drill and agreed with Jason without a second thought. They quickly dismounted. Bret and Teddy paid little attention. Come hell or high water, they were going to make it to the stand of trees before them.

In an instant, big drops of rain began to fall by the bucketful. A loud clap of thunder boomed so close it almost knocked Jason to the ground. In the same instant, a bolt of lightning lit up the darkened sky. Another one followed right behind the first. Thunder was crashing and lightning flashing all around them. Jason, Pat and Owen held their position until the storm and the danger had passed. When they felt it was safe, the three stood up and assured each other that they were OK. In the distance they heard what sounded like rolling thunder, but soon realized it was the sound of a thousand or more cows, spooked and running for their lives. Not a word needed to be spoken. No one envied the drovers that belonged to that herd.

A once-dry gully close to where they stood was now a raging river. Although spooked, the three horses were still tied down and alive. They walked them until they settled down and then mounted up and headed toward the trees hoping Teddy and Bret had made it safely. Luck was with them, as they had, and were patiently waiting for the others.

'We thought you guys were goners,' exclaimed Teddy.

'Us?' questioned Jason. 'Running for cover like that was a really stupid thing to do. You could have gotten yourselves killed.'

Teddy's temperament was already spread thin, so the comment didn't sit well with him. 'What the hell do you know?' he remarked. 'We made it just fine.'

'I know plenty about these storms and I'll stick to what I just said. That was a stupid thing to do. You should have gotten off your horse. You can't outrun lightning.'

'Well we did, and more than one at that. You don't know shit,' replied Teddy.

'OK you two, let it go,' interjected Owen. 'Let's get moving.'

Teddy refused to let it go, and for the next couple of days he continued to pick at Jason every chance he got. He made fun of the way he rode, his Midwest accent, even the color of his hair. Finally Jason had had enough. Teddy was making some wisecrack statement about his hat as Jason rode up next to him and without warning, shoved him off his horse.

Teddy's boot caught in the stirrup and his horse began to drag him. Luckily Bret was close enough to grab the horse and bring it to a halt. Teddy worked his boot free and made a beeline for Jason, who jumped from his horse toward Teddy and took him to the ground. Teddy put a move on Jason and managed to get in a good lick to the side of his head.

Jason didn't take kindly to that and came back at Teddy with two strong punches to his stomach and one crushing blow to his nose. But that didn't stop Teddy. He grabbed Jason and the two were back on the ground. Owen finally stepped in and pulled them apart.

'What in the hell is the matter with the two of you?' he yelled.

'I've had more than my share of his teasing. I put up with it for a while, but no more,' replied Jason as he began to brush himself off.

'If you can't handle it, why don't you just go your own way? We don't need your kind in Texas anyway,' shouted Teddy as he grabbed up his hat from the ground.

'My kind? What do you mean by that?'

'You know damn well what I mean,' replied Teddy. 'You're a no-good Northerner. Why don't you stay in Kansas? We don't want you down in Texas.'

Jason was stunned. He wasn't expecting to hear that from Teddy. 'Fine,' replied Jason. 'I'll go my own way.' He grabbed up his hat, mounted his horse and started to ride off.

'Wait,' came the cry from behind him. He turned to see Pat riding his way. 'I'm going with you,' she stated.

Bret objected. 'No way in hell are you going with him, Pat. I told your pa I'd watch after you. If I don't bring you back, I'm as good as dead.'

'You tell him I'll be along shortly,' replied Pat. 'He might whup you, but he won't kill you.'

'No, you're coming with me.' Bret dismounted and started toward her. Jason put a quick stop to his advance as he drew his gun on him. Bret stopped in his tracks. Teddy and Owen set their hands on their revolvers, ready to draw if it came down to it.

Pat drew her gun and pointed it at Bret. 'Don't come any closer, Bret. I'm going with Jason. Tell my pa what I just told you. I'll be along shortly.'

Owen interjected. 'Now hold on here just a minute. This is getting way out of hand. Put those guns away. That isn't necessary here. Patricia O'Donnell, your father allowed you to be part of this outfit with the express stipulation that you abide by what we determine to be in your best interest, and by God, this is not it. We need you now, more than ever, so quit this foolishness and get back over here. And Jason, there's no need for you to be running off like this. So you got into a scuffle with Teddy. He ain't a bad kid, just a little abrasive at times. We've all learned to have thick skin around him. Just let it go and I'll make sure he keeps his mouth shut.'

Owen looked over at Teddy and with a tone that sounded more like an order, he asked, 'Ain't that right, Teddy?'

Teddy didn't say a word, he just turned his horse and rode off.

Bret threw up his hands in disgust. 'I'm done babysitting you. I'll shoot your pa before I let him lay a hand on me on account of you.' He mounted and rode off to catch up with Teddy.

Owen continued to try and talk some sense into both Jason and Pat, but neither of them wanted to hear any part of it. Finally he gave up trying as well. 'OK, have it your way. I'll tell your pa you'll be along shortly. I'll make sure Bret won't have to shoot him. You just make damn sure you show up ... and I mean shortly,' he insisted.

With that he turned and rode after Teddy and Bret.

Jason and Pat watched as they rode out of sight.

'Now what?' asked Pat.

'Now we head to Texas,' replied Jason.

The two rode on, keeping a wide distance from any cattle coming their way.

'I've never seen so many cows,' exclaimed Jason. 'We see a herd or two every single day. Are they all coming out of Texas?' he asked.

'Most are,' replied Pat. 'Cattle are pretty much worthless down south. You can raise them cheap. Then walk them up the road to Kansas where they're worth ten times more, and make a big profit for your trouble. This is the second time my pa has sent cattle up to Wichita.'

'So what's the thing with Owen? How did he end up in charge of you all, and why did he say he needs you more than ever?' asked Jason.

'Owen? Owen is my pa's *Segundo* back home. He was put in charge of the drive and he's the one carrying the money from the sale of the herd.'

Jason gave Pat a sideways glance as if trying to figure her out. 'You had the responsibility of helping protect that money and you walked away from it?' he questioned.

'I'm not needed as much as Owen thinks I am. He was just trying to get me to go with them,' replied Pat.

Jason thought he had Pat figured out, but the fact that she was not honor bound disturbed him, especially when there was so much at stake.

That evening Jason and Pat made camp in a grassy area under a grove of cottonwood trees. The night air was cool and they talked for a time next to the fire, but soon the conversation died down along with the fire. Suddenly without warning, Pat straddled

Jason's legs and sat on his lap facing him. She took off her hat and let her long hair fall around her shoulders. She then brushed back Jason's hat and ran her thin fingers through his hair, then laid her wet lips on his.

'I've thought about this moment for days,' she whispered.

Jason gave no resistance as she pushed him on to his back.

Owen, Teddy and Bret continued on. Teddy nursed his wounds as Bret fumed and fretted about Pat and what her pa was going to do to him when he found out she didn't come back with them. Owen tried to console him. 'Don't worry about it, Bret. I'll take the responsibility. I'm the one in charge. Let's just make sure we get this money home safe. If we lose it, we're all dead men.'

'This whole mess could have been avoided if we had just put a bullet in Jason. I would much rather shoot him as Pat's pa,' remarked Bret.

Teddy chimed in. 'I'll agree to that. I'm all for turning around and finding the little runt.'

'Little runt?' questioned Owen. 'That little runt sure bloodied your nose good.'

'Lucky punch,' replied Teddy. 'It would never happen again.'

'Well just the same, let's have no more talk about

killin' someone. It ain't right.'

'He's a no-good Yank,' scoffed Teddy.

'That was your daddy's war, not yours,' replied Owen.

'It was your war too, Owen. Don't you feel the same?' asked Teddy.

'I don't hold no grudges. It ain't my way. I've seen way too much hate in the eyes of men. More than enough to last me the rest of my life. It's a worthless emotion and the cause of most of the troubles in this world. I would suggest you get over it while you're still young and healthy.'

Owen moved up ahead of the two boys. He had said his piece and now wanted to reset the pace.

Teddy and Bret talked between themselves. They liked Owen, but didn't necessarily share his point of view when it came to Northerners, or Jason McKinney for that matter.

'There has got to be a way to get Pat away from Jason. I don't understand why she went with him in the first place?' questioned Bret.

'I guess she got tired of us,' replied Teddy with a wide grin.

Bret glanced over at Teddy and smiled. 'I think you may be right,' he remarked. 'And by the way, your nose looks like hell.'

'It feels like hell too,' grimaced Teddy.

As they rode along, Bret suggested to Teddy that

they have a little fun with Owen. 'Follow my lead,' he said to Teddy.

The two boys rode up alongside of Owen. 'Say, Owen,' said Bret inquisitively, 'you know what we should do to keep that money you're carrying even more safe than it is right now?'

'And what might that be?' inquired Owen.

'I think you should divide it up into three parts and give Teddy and me each a part.'

'That's a very good idea,' added Teddy. 'If something happens to one of us at least two-thirds of the money would be safe. If something were to happen to you, all the money could be lost.'

'This money belongs to the Square D, and I'm in charge of it; besides, there ain't nothing going to happen to me . . . unless one of you plan to make it happen,' answered Owen with a slight hint of concern.

'We ain't planning on doing anything, Owen. But it's like what Teddy said, we just want to make sure all the money doesn't get lost,' answered Bret.

'OK, OK,' replied Owen. 'I get it. You two are foolin' with me . . . right?'

Teddy and Bret couldn't hold back their laughter any longer. 'Of course we are, Owen. You should know that. It's a long ride home and we're just having some fun.'

'You had me worried there for a second,' admitted

Owen. 'But only for a second.'

The three men rode on. It was still early and it had already been one hell of a day.

CHAPTER 4

RABBIT RUN

With each passing day, Jason was growing fonder of Pat. She was a tease, but Jason – who had never been exposed to a meaningful relationship before – didn't get it. He thought she was just the playful type and that her feelings for him were as genuine as his were for her. They did indeed enjoy each other's company, and conversations between the two were genuine and sometimes deep. Pat was quite the talker and for someone so young, she seemed to know a lot about the world and the ways of it. Jason thought he was genuinely beginning to fall in love.

Pat on the other hand knew exactly what she was up to, and love had nothing to do with it. She wasn't the type to fall in love. She was all about having a good time. Her birth name was Patricia, but her father had no use for a girl. He needed a man to help around the ranch and he put her to the task. He took to calling her Pat and it caught on with the rest of the hands around the ranch. They all took a liking to her, not only because she could hold her own with the daily chores or in playful banter. And not because she could easily put a man to shame in a full-blown argument, no, the real reason was because . . . well let's just say that among most of the men, she had acquired the nickname of 'rabbit' for obvious reasons. And that was the very reason she took to Jason, and no other.

Pat tried not to get too far behind Owen and the others. She knew she would have to ride in with them. There was no way around it. To this, Jason had no clue.

They traveled through Oklahoma and crossed the border into Texas less than a day's ride to the small town of Wichita Falls. Pat had been there in the past and wanted to pass it by. It came up in conversation one evening as they sat near the fire. Pat tried to play it down as a dirty little hole in the road and not worth taking the slight detour needed to get there, but Jason had other ideas.

'I think we need to head over to Wichita Falls, Pat,' suggested Jason. 'It may just be a hole in the road,

but it's some place where we can pick up a few supplies.'

'We don't need any supplies. It's only another four
days' ride. I'm sure we can make it to Dallas without
stopping,' suggested Pat.

She was really against stopping. She knew Owen
and the others would be showing up at the ranch
soon and she needed to be with them. The detour
would make it that much more difficult to catch up.

Jason wouldn't take no for an answer. 'If it's four
more days, we need some supplies. We're heading to
Wichita Falls. Besides, it's been a month of Sundays
since I've slept in a real bed or had a beer, and if you
can hold your own like you say you can, we'll make a
night of it.'

With that settled, they made camp for the night,
and the following morning they rode into town just
as the sun was beginning to peek over the horizon.

They stabled their horses and found a room with a
clean bed. There was also a room where one could
take a bath. After stowing their gear they walked
down to a local café for a real breakfast of coffee, biscuits and gravy, eggs over easy and a juicy chunk of
steak. It had been a couple of weeks since they had
eaten that good. They both enjoyed the meal and lingered longer than they had anticipated. They talked
about riding on to the ranch and up to the house
together where she would introduce him to her

father. Jason wasn't too keen on that idea, but knew it would have to be done.

'I think your father will probably shoot me, to be honest with you,' he told Pat.

'My father is very understanding, Jason,' replied Pat. 'He'll welcome you with open arms. I guarantee it.'

Jason wasn't too sure, but Pat knew her father and he was learning to trust her. 'Well, if you're sure about it, then that's what we'll do.'

Pat suggested they go pick up the supplies they needed. Jason thanked the waitress and Pat complimented the cook on the biscuits and gravy as they headed out the door to get their supplies.

The store was small, but it carried all the essentials they would need to get them to the Square D. They walked the supplies back to the room and Jason lay down on the bed.

'I haven't had a meal like that in quite some time. I think I overdid it. My stomach feels like shit.'

Pat sounded genuinely sympathetic when she insisted that he lay back and sleep it off while she went downstairs and took a bath. Jason agreed and closed his eyes. Within ten minutes he was sound asleep. Pat was deliberately slow and silent as she picked up the supplies they had just purchased and slipped out of the room. Jason shifted on the bed, but never woke.

Pat knew she needed to hurry. A bath would take about an hour and by the time Jason figured out that she had run off she hoped to have a two-hour lead on him. She said hello to the man at the front desk as she headed out the door and straight to the livery. She settled up her bill and gave the man another six dollars to re-shoe Jason's horse with the stipulation that he needed to hold off on it for one hour. The owner of the livery was quick to catch on. He had a good idea as to what was taking place.

'So you're running from the man you rode in with and you want me to slow him up some, is that how it is?'

Pat looked at the man with a hesitant smile. 'Why yes, that's exactly how it is,' she replied.

'For another five dollars I'll hold him off for as long as I possibly can.'

Pat liked the idea and paid the man without so much as a grimace. 'Thank you,' she said as she headed out. She put the horse into an easy canter and as soon as she felt it was ready, she took him to a full gallop and made a beeline for the Square D, hoping to catch up with Owen and the others before they reached the ranch.

Jason slept for close to two hours. When he woke, Pat wasn't in the room. He didn't know for sure what time it was, so he thought he'd wander down to the front desk and see if he could find her. He wasn't fully awake yet and didn't notice that the supplies were gone.

The clerk behind the desk had his reading glasses pulled down along his nose as he was looking over the town paper. It was a weekly edition and the clerk was chuckling about a story that had been posted. He looked up at Jason. 'Says here in the paper that President Grant may pay our fair city a visit in the near future. Where does this information come from anyhow? President Grant will never set foot in Texas, let alone Wichita Falls, I can almost guarantee that.' He chuckled one more time before asking Jason what he could do for him.

'I'm wondering if the gal I came in here with is done with her bath yet?'

'Bath? She didn't take no bath. She came down the stairs and headed straight out the door,' replied the clerk as he laid the paper down on the desk in front of him.

Jason was a bit confused. 'No bath?'

'No bath,' echoed the clerk as he gestured toward the street. 'She went straight out the door.'

Jason walked out the door and stood on the boardwalk, not sure where to look next. *Maybe I should just wait for her to show up*, he thought. Not knowing where she might have gone, he decided against waiting and walked over to the livery in hopes that she might have gone to check on the horses.

As he entered the stable, he noticed that Pat's horse was missing. 'Have you seen the gal I rode in with?' he asked the stableman.

'I saw her a couple of hours ago. She picked up her horse and left,' he replied as he continued raking out one of the stalls.

'Left? Did she say where she was going?'

His answer was short. 'Nope.'

Jason was becoming more confused by the minute. It was beginning to look like he had been left behind. But for the life of him, he couldn't figure out why. Maybe she had second thoughts about introducing him to her father. Maybe it was all a big mistake, he thought. Maybe she. . . . He stopped himself. *Maybe I just need to find her and ask her. It's the only way I'll know for sure just what the hell is going on here.*

Jason hurried back to his room to get his supplies. She had a good jump on him but he felt he could catch her before she made it back to the Square D. He was already in a foul mood and when he realized she had taken all the supplies, he became furious. He began to yell and curse, he threw things across the room. Jason was making such a ruckus that the clerk became concerned enough to pound on the door.

'What!' screamed Jason in a fit of rage.

The clerk shouted through the door. 'Sir, I don't know what's going on in there, but you have got to keep it down. I have other guests here and if you insist on continuing in this manner, I'll be forced to call the sheriff . . . and if you've broken anything, you can expect to pay for it when you settle up your bill.'

Jason pulled the door open so quickly it startled the clerk. He pushed past him and headed for the door. 'I'm going for some supplies. I'll be back,' he stated as he quickly headed for the door.

The clerk didn't trust him. 'I think you need to pay your bill now,' he shouted.

Jason kept going without acknowledging the clerk. He headed straight for the mercantile and began to gather the supplies he needed for the trail. It was only a few minutes before the sheriff darkened the door. He wasn't a particularly impressive-looking man. Not big and burly, no fancy guns or clothes. He was just an average-looking man but he carried his badge well, meaning that when he walked up to you on official business, you instinctively knew he wasn't about to tolerate any tomfoolery. He was a person who commanded respect, and most would instinctively give it to him. But not Jason.

Without hesitation, he headed straight for Jason with an introduction. 'How do you do, young man. I'm Sheriff Bodie. I understand you were creating quite a ruckus at the boarding house a few minutes ago. What seems to be your trouble and how may I be of assistance to you?'

'I'm fine and I don't need your assistance,' replied Jason. 'I'm getting a few supplies and then I'll be on my way.'

'On your way to where?' asked the sheriff.

'On my way out of town. Where I go from there is my own damn business.' Jason's tone was less than cordial, which the sheriff took note of.

'I do hope you're planning on stopping back by the boarding house to pay your bill, and any other encumbrances you may have incurred during your recent bout of unwelcome behavior,' Bodie ventured, his tone bordering on the sarcastic.

Jason wasn't following and was a bit perplexed at the sheriff's official sounding language. 'Encumbrances?' he questioned.

'Yes, your bill and any damages you may have caused to your room. The clerk will have the bill waiting for you when you get there,' replied the sheriff. 'In fact, I think I'll just tag along to make sure you get there safely.'

'I don't need your escort, and I'm not planning on going back there just yet,' remarked Jason angrily as he finished gathering his supplies.

The sheriff wasn't going to tolerate Jason's attitude any longer. 'You may not need the escort, but you're getting it just the same, and as far as your plans go, they just changed. You can either accompany me back to the boarding house or my jailhouse. The choice is yours.'

Jason's eyes widened at the man's tone. 'I've done nothing that would give you cause to see me as a dishonest person, so just keep your distance from me. I'll get there when I get there. You can watch me from a distance if you so choose, but I don't need an escort,' Jason walked up to the counter to pay for his supplies. 'See here, I'm paying my bill. When I finish here, I'll go pay the clerk, then I'll go pay the stableman and then I'll be on my way.'

He pushed past the sheriff and stomped out of the store in a huff. The sheriff followed close behind without saying a word. He wasn't interested in arresting Jason, he just wanted the kid with the bad attitude out of his town.

Jason did as he said. He stopped by the boarding house to settle the bill. The clerk was waiting at the desk and the sheriff gave Jason his space and waited outside on the boardwalk.

'What do I owe you?' asked Jason sharply.

The clerk handed Jason a slip of paper with the bill and the cost of the damages Jason had caused to the room. 'Ten dollars? That seems a little steep considering I didn't even use the bed.'

'You still rented the room for the night, and this also includes a charge for the broken bowl and water pitcher, and the torn curtains you pulled off the window,' stated the clerk.

Jason angrily threw fifteen dollars down on to the counter. 'Here's your money and here's an extra five dollars.'

'What's this for?' asked the clerk.

'For this lamp I accidentally knocked on to the floor,' replied Jason.

The clerk was perplexed. 'What lamp?'

'This one,' replied Jason as he took a wide swipe at the gas lamp sitting on the counter. It crashed to the floor and shattered into pieces. The guest book and other papers followed close behind.

'Get the hell out of this building, you little bastard!' demanded the clerk.

Jason purposefully stepped out on to the board-walk and headed directly toward the livery.

The sheriff, hearing the commotion, stuck his head in the door. 'Is there a problem with the kid paying his bill?' asked the sheriff.

The clerk was just stepping around the counter. 'No problem with the bill, but. . . .'

'Good,' replied the sheriff as he quickly turned away in order to catch up with Jason. The clerk's final words hung heavy in the air, never reaching the sheriff's ear.

Jason walked swiftly to the livery stable and settled the bill. He wasted little time saddling his horse. He mounted up, and as he left the stable the sheriff greeted him, touching the brim of his hat in a mock salute. 'Sorry for your trouble. Try to enjoy the rest of your day.'

Jason flashed an angry look at the sheriff. 'Go to hell!' he growled as he spurred his horse and headed out of town.

The sheriff shrugged it off and went back to his other duties, and the stableman went back to spreading straw. He chuckled to himself. *Never did re-shoe that horse. It didn't need it.*

When Jason rode out he was mad and angry at the world. He rode hard for what seemed like an hour, thinking he was going to catch up to Pat. She, on the other hand, had no intention of being caught by Jason. Her intention was to catch up to Owen and the others before they got back to the ranch.

Jason's horse was getting winded so he reluctantly decided it would be best to slow down. His horse needed to rest and his anger was beginning to cool to the point where he could finally begin to reason with himself. He was finally starting to see it. Pat had used him until she grew tired of him. It was the suddenness of her leaving that really took him by surprise. *Why in the world would I want her back?* he thought. He liked Pat, she was fun and playful, but he knew now it was all for her own amusement. As Jason made more sense of it, he reined in his horse and sat there facing south. He gave his situation some hard thought.

'Well I've been to Texas and I can't hardly say I like it.' He finally turned around and started riding back to Kansas.

Pat knew she needed to catch up with Owen and the others before they reached the Square D. They were almost a full day's ride ahead of her, so she kept a fast pace hoping to catch them within two days. She wasn't comfortable spending her nights under the stars alone and decided not to kindle a fire for fear that someone would see it. A stranger trying to enter her camp would not be to her liking.

The next couple of days had her wondering if she was even on the same trail as the others. She kept on, knowing that she could at least make it back to the ranch. Riding in alone would not be ideal for her or the men she was supposed to be with, so she kept a sharp eye out as she rode. It was evening on the second night and Pat had found a nice spot among some cottonwood trees to camp for the evening. In the distance she could see the faint flicker of a fire. She wondered if it might be Owen and the others. Early in the morning she would head in that direction, but stay far enough back to not bring attention to herself. Hopefully she'd be able to see from a distance who it might be.

Pat broke camp before sunup. As she closed in on the camp she had seen the night before, the fire had already been rekindled. She got as close as she dared with her horse and decided to tie him off and move in closer on foot. Before she was close enough to make out faces, she could hear voices. It was Bret and Owen, she was sure of it. She went back and retrieved her horse and rode up to the camp, Owen caught sight of someone coming close. He pulled his gun and called out. 'Who goes there?'

Pat called back, 'It's me, Owen, Pat.'

Owen called back. 'Pat? Pat who? I don't know anyone named Pat.'

'Stop joking with me, Owen and let me come in,' Pat protested. 'I could use some hot coffee.'

Owen holstered his gun. 'Well, come on in then. You're the last person in the world I expected to see this morning.'

As Pat rode into camp Bret grabbed her horse by the bridle. 'You sure know how to scare the hell out of a person. Do you realize I've shot your pa about a hundred times in my mind?'

'Where's your lover?' asked Teddy sarcastically.

Before Pat could answer, Owen spoke up, and he was not in a good mood. 'Pat, none of us men are happy with what you did. If you think you can just ride in here and things are going to be as if nothing happened, you've got another guess coming. If we're all to keep the wrath of your pa off us, then you need us and we need you. It ain't gonna be a pleasant ride from here on out. Just keep in line and we'll all make it back without gettin' an ass whippin'. Is that clear?'

Pat agreed, and the four of them rode on home together. Even though the three men were all curious, no one asked about Jason, but they all kept a close watch, just in case he decided to show up.

CHAPTER 5

CLOSING IN

It was a miserable sun-scorched July afternoon and shade was in short supply. The streets were all but empty of both man and beast. The stranger went unnoticed as he rode into town. He was tall, stocky and in need of a shave. He was a man on a mission that took him straight to Sheriff Mason's office. Finding him in, he closed the door and latched it. Mason stood up with his hand on his gun as the door closed.

'No need for that, Sheriff. My name is Dan Danner, I'm a US Marshal and I'm here on official business.' The marshal flashed his badge at Sheriff Mason and took a seat across the desk.

Without saying a word, Sheriff Mason walked back

over to the door and opened it, then walked back to his desk and sat down. 'It's a might humid here today, marshal. I'm trying to catch a breeze. What can I do for you?'

'I'm here to serve a warrant and take into custody a man by the name of Mac Shepard.'

Sheriff Mason almost fell back in his chair when he heard the name. 'Mac Shepard? What on earth is he being charged with?'

'Cattle rustling,' replied the marshal. 'He was involved in setting up the theft, and directly involved in the purchase and sale of some 200 head last fall.'

Sheriff Mason stroked his chin as he thought back to when he and Miles had this very conversation. 'Well if that don't beat all. I guess Miles was right after all.'

'Miles, who's Miles?' questioned Marshal Danner.

'That would be Miles Hanley, a local rancher. He suspected Mac all along, but I had no proof. My hands were tied.'

'Well, I have the proof,' replied Danner, his voice revealing a little cockiness.

'How so?' questioned the sheriff.

Marshal Danner continued. 'Seems the two men who actually did the rustling got into a drunken brawl over a woman up in Abilene. Seems one of the men shot the other, but before the man died he decided to get even with his killer. He spilled the beans on a rustling job the two men did for a man named Mac Shepard in Fort Scott. Said there was a train ready and waiting for them. They loaded the cattle and the train went on its way. They got their money and did the same.'

'That's interesting,' replied Mason. 'Miles said he heard a train. I figured he was hearing something off in the distance. Did your investigation follow up on the train? I'd be curious to know how that was possible.'

'It did,' replied Danner. 'The stationmaster had no record of a train in the area. But that doesn't rule it out. It only means we don't have all the facts yet, and who knows, we may not get them all. What we do have is a deathbed confession with witnesses and that's about all I need.'

'One more question. Was there any mention of a kid named Jason?' quizzed Mason.

'Yes, there was,' answered Danner. 'I questioned the man who did the shooting. I admit I had to rough him up a bit, but he finally came clean. Seems they picked up a kid named Jason along the trail. He agreed to give them a hand. Apparently the kid had no clue the cattle were stolen. I pushed pretty hard to get him to tell me the truth about the kid. It makes no sense to me that he wouldn't have known, but he insisted that they never filled him in and the kid had no clue. My guess is he was protecting him for some unknown reason. In any case, I'm not after the kid, just Mac Shepard.'

'So what's your plan?' asked Mason.

Danner shrugged. 'Right now, I'm hungry and tired. I'm going to get a bath and a shave, then I'm getting myself some supper. I'll meet you back here in the morning. We'll ride out to Max Shepard's place. I'll serve the warrant and make the arrest. I'll need you to back me up in case he or his men give us any trouble.'

Sheriff Mason shifted in his chair. 'If you're thinking there might be gunplay, I doubt if that'll be the case. Mac Shepard doesn't seem the type.'

Danner leaned across the desk and looked Mason square in the eye. He was direct and to the point. 'Don't underestimate what a man will do when his life is on the line. Most men would rather take their chances with a bullet, when the alternative is swinging from the end of a rope. I don't expect Shepard to be any different, and you shouldn't either. You're backing me up, so expect it.' And with that, Danner pulled himself erect. 'I'll be here in the morning, around seven o'clock. Be ready to go.'

Sheriff Mason didn't bother to get out of his chair as Danner walked out in search of a bath and a shave. Mason didn't like the fact that Danner was giving the orders in *his* office.

*

The following morning Marshal Danner was up early. A good breakfast was always the first thing on his agenda and this morning was no different. He had easily found the local café and was waiting at the door when it opened. The smell of fresh brewed coffee filled the room as he took a seat at the counter. Today was an official business day, which meant his badge was pinned to the outside of his vest.

The waitress gave him a courteous smile as she placed a cup of hot coffee on the counter. Marshal Danner liked the service already.

The door opened and in walked Andrew Crocker, who proceeded to sit down right next to the lawman. He couldn't help but notice the badge. 'Good morning, marshal. My name is Andrew, Reverend Andrew Crocker. What brings you to town this morning? Are you on official business, or just taking in the sights?'

'Official business,' replied the marshal as he took a sip of his coffee. Ignoring Andrew and looking toward the waitress, he commented. 'Good coffee ma'am. I'd like to order some hotcakes and bacon.'

Andrew Crocker continued his inquiry. 'Might I ask what your official business might be?'

'I don't believe you're an official of this town.' replied Danner.

'I was the pastor in this town for many years and these good people were my flock. I still care deeply for them and if one of them is in trouble, I may want to be there to minister in any way I can.'

'Maybe you should leave the ministering to the new preacher, and the questioning to the town officials,' replied Danner sharply.

Andrew's eyes narrowed and he smiled, the warmth failing to reach his eyes. 'I'm still a man of God and I do have my ear to the ground, or should I say to the heavens, so to speak. My guess is Mac Shepard might be involved in your official duties, but that's only a guess.'

Surprised at the comment, Danner questioned Andrew. 'And what do you know of Mac Shepard?'

'I know Mac Shepard has his weaknesses like most of the men in this town. I'm not his judge. If the laws of man see fit to bind him, so be it. God and the courts will deal fairly with him.' Andrew took a sip from the coffee the waitress had given him.

'You have a sound ear and a bit of wisdom about you, Mr. Crocker. I recommend you not say a word about this conversation,' suggested Danner.

The waitress placed a plate of hotcakes and bacon in front of Danner and he quickly took a big bite. He could feel the preacher's eyes on him.

Andrew pried a little deeper. 'Since we've established the subject of this conversation to be Mac Shepard, might I inquire as to what his charge might be?'

'No,' replied Danner bluntly, as he easily shoved a whole strip of bacon into his mouth.

Andrew didn't let up. 'Well then, I would venture to guess it has something to do with cattle rustling.'

Danner almost choked on the bacon he was chewing. 'How in the hell do you know that?' he loudly demanded.

'I not only know their weaknesses, I also know their sins.' Andrew Crocker took another gulp of his coffee, got up and stepped toward the door. He looked toward the waitress and pointed at Danner. 'He'll pay.'

Danner looked surprised and held his hands out palms up in a dumbfounded gesture.

'Don't worry about it, marshal. His coffee is always on the house,' stated the waitress. She stepped into the kitchen and told the cook to stall Danner and that she would only be a minute. She took off her apron and stepped out the back door.

The doctor's office was only a block away. The waitress raced down the street as fast as she dared, but not so fast as to bring attention to herself. She was glad to find the door unlocked. She quickly entered and found Dr. Dunn getting ready for the day, as he had just arrived. 'Where's Sarah?' she hastily asked.

'Sarah's out at her brother's today,' he replied. Discerning a sense of urgency in her voice, he asked, 'May I help you?'

'You have to get an urgent message to her,' the waitress implored. 'There's a marshal in town. He's on his way to Mac's place to arrest him for cattle rustling.'

Ben was surprised to hear this. 'Surely you must be mistaken. Mac's not a cattle rustler.'

The waitress continued. 'Listen, Doctor Dunn. Sarah and Mac are my friends. I hope you're right and this is all one big mistake, but this is what I know. There's a marshal sitting in the café right now who plans to arrest Mac for cattle rustling. Someone needs to warn him.'

'All right,' replied Ben. 'I'll take care of it. I'll ride out there and give Mac a heads up. Thanks for letting me know.'

'Thank you, Doctor Dunn. I really do appreciate it.'

The waitress left the office and headed back to the café. 'Good morning again,' she said to Andrew Crocker as she whizzed passed him.

Andrew just smiled. He knew exactly what she was up to.

The waitress returned through the back door of the café just as the marshal was finishing his second piece of fresh apple pie.

'Did you make this pie, ma'am?' he inquired.

'Why, yes I did, marshal. Do you like it?'

'Best pie I ever ate,' Danner stated as he washed

down the last bite with a swig of hot coffee. 'What's your secret?'

'Well if I told you it wouldn't be a secret now, would it?' she teased.

'I guess you're right about that,' replied Danner. 'I'd love it if my wife could bake a pie like this.' He pulled some money from his pocket to pay his bill.

'But just for you,' the waitress continued. 'I'm going to tell you my secret. In fact, I'll write it down just for your wife. It has to do with . . .'

She stalled Danner for another twenty minutes.

As the waitress delayed the marshal, Miles Hanley, who happened to be in town, crossed paths with Andrew, who had taken a seat in an empty chair in front of the barbershop.

'I never did thank you for those words you gave me, Andrew,' said Miles as he sat down next to the man and leaned the back of his chair against the wall. 'I'm hoping they did the trick.'

'There's no trick involved,' replied Andrew, as he kept his focus on the café down the street. 'I'm sure Mac dwelled on those words, and as the Good Book says, "he who dwelleth upon the word of the Lord will receive the desires of his heart". What he's been thinking about for the past few months is coming into being for him.'

'Well, however it is, I hope it worked,' answered Miles. 'You seem to have a knack for judging people.'

Andrew turned his attention off the café and on to Miles. 'I judge no man. I merely plant the seeds.'

'Well, you would have made one hell of a farmer,' chided Miles.

'I'm a shepherd,' Andrew replied, clearly unhappy with the comment.

'You also got a way with words. Once Mac is arrested, his ranch will be left unattended. What words can you give me that'll help me get my hands on it?'

Clearly unhappy, Andrew looked at Miles with intensity and pointed a stern finger at him. 'Thou shalt not covet, and if those words won't work for you, try these ... go to hell.' Andrew got up and angrily walked away, leaving Miles to wonder what he had said to cause the retired parson to get so upset.

Benjamin Dunn closed the office and saddled up his horse. He always kept it hitched behind the office for those times when he needed it quickly. This was one of those times. He rode like the wind out to Mac's place. There was an eeriness about this ride. It reminded him of the night he left Virginia with a mob of angry vigilantes on his heels.

He reached the ranch in record time, but there was already another horse out front. Was he too late? Sarah heard him coming and met him at the door. 'Ben, what are you doing here? Is everything all right? What's going on?'

Without giving Ben a chance to reply she grabbed him by the arm and pulled him through the doorway. 'I'm so glad you're here. Look what the cat drug in.'

As Ben was pulled into the house he saw Jason sitting at the kitchen table. 'Well I'll be darned,' he exclaimed. Jason stood up and the two shook hands. 'You look a little older, Jason.'

'I've grown some,' he replied.

'So Ben, why are you here?' inquired Sarah.

'Is Mac here?' he asked.

'No, 'she replied. 'He left for Mound City this morning. You're starting to worry me, Ben. What's going on?'

'Sarah, I'm afraid I have some distressing news. There's a marshal in town and word is he's on his way here to arrest Mac for rustling cattle.'

'Rustling cattle? There must be some mistake. Mac is no cattle rustler. He owns all of his cows. He didn't take them from anyone. I'm sure he can explain, right?'

'I'm not sure what the truth is, Sarah. I'm just going by what I've been told.'

Sarah turned to Jason. Her eyes fixed on his. 'Jason, do you know anything about this?'

Jason dropped his head. He couldn't hold her gaze. 'These cows are his, but it's not my place to explain the past deeds of my father,' he replied. 'But I will warn him.'

Sarah just stood there looking at Jason in disbelief. 'What do you mean, past deeds?'

Jason grabbed his hat. 'I need a few supplies.' He went to the pantry and took whatever was available and stuffed them into a bag. He gave Sarah a hug.

'You didn't answer my question,' the woman scolded. She knew it would be pointless to push him.

'I'll be back,' Jason stated assuredly as he again skirted the question. He shook Ben's hand. 'Thanks for the warning.' He left the house and mounted up.

'He took the old road,' shouted Sarah. 'It's safer.'

After Jason rode off, Sarah broke down and began to weep. Ben held her close.

The lawman carefully folded the piece of paper and put it in his breast pocket. 'My wife's a good cook. I know she'll enjoy giving this recipe a try.' Danner got up to leave. 'Well, you've kept me longer than I planned, so I've really got to get out of here.' The marshal paid his bill and hurried out the door. The pie was good, but now he was wondering if he should have eaten that second piece. He walked over to the sheriff's office.

It was past eight o'clock when the marshal darkened the sheriff's door. 'Sorry I'm late. The café down the street serves a good breakfast, and their pie is first rate.'

'Oh, I know about the pie,' replied the sheriff. 'More than once I've indulged myself with a second piece. Especially the apple. It's usually a bad idea, at least for me. But it's so damn good, I can't help myself. I end up having to do some quick-steppin', if you know what I mean. Are you ready to go?'

'Will be in just a minute,' replied Danner. His discomfort level was growing by the minute. 'I need to step out back first.'

The sheriff chuckled. 'You must have had the apple.'

'Twice,' replied Danner as he headed out the back door. When he had finished with his emergency situation he pulled the recipe from his pocket and threw it down the hole.

As soon as the two men were ready, they saddled up and headed toward Mac Shepard's place. The ride was slow. Danner had to make one more 'Apple pie stop' along the way. Sheriff Mason was in no hurry. He was anything but anxious about what they were about to do. He actually liked Mac and his sister, Sarah. Mac would stand trial and if he was found guilty he would more than likely hang. And with Sarah about to be wed to Dr. Dunn, it would make for a truly unhappy wedding.

As they approached the ranch, Marshal Danner laid out the plan. 'Sheriff, I'll serve the warrant alone. I'll need you to stay mounted with the horses. If Mac should try to run, I'll need you to head him off. Don't let him get to a horse. I really don't want to have to chase him.'

Sheriff Mason easily agreed. He really didn't want to be involved in this any more than he had to. He didn't relish the thought of looking Mac or Sarah in the face when the arrest was being made.

As they approached, they could see one horse out front. 'Don't let anyone get to that horse,' ordered Danner.

They stopped just outside the front gate. The marshal made one last check. He had his badge, gun and paperwork. He dismounted, took a deep breath and walked up to the front door. He knocked loudly.

Dr Dunn opened the front door.

'Mac Shepard?' asked the marshal in an official tone.

'No, my name is Ben Dunn.'

'Is Mac Shepard in the house or here on the ranch somewhere?'

'No,' replied Ben.

'My name is Marshal Dan Danner and I'm looking for Mac Shepard. May I ask you to please step outside? I'd like the sheriff here to identify you, if you don't mind.' He pointed toward the sheriff.

'No, not at all,' replied Ben as he stepped outside.

The marshal called out to the sheriff. 'Sheriff

Mason, can you please identify this man for me?'

Sheriff Mason called back. 'That's not Mac, that's Doctor Ben Dunn.'

Marshal Danner then asked Ben, 'Can you tell me where I can find Mac Shepard.'

'What's this all about, marshal?' asked Ben.

'This is official business. I have an arrest warrant for Mac Shepard,' he replied.

Ben acted surprised. 'Arrest warrant? What on earth for?'

Marshal Danner ignored the question. 'Do you know where I can locate Mr Shepard?'

'He's gone on business and won't be back for a couple of days,' replied Ben.

'And where did he go?' asked the marshal with a note of skepticism.

'Mound City,' replied Ben.

'Are you the only one here?' asked the marshal.

'No, my fiancée is here, as well as two hired hands. Do you need the sheriff to identify them as well? The men are out right now and won't be back until suppertime.'

'May I have your word that Mac Shepard is not on the ranch?' questioned the marshal.

'You have my word,' replied Ben.

The marshal turned toward Sheriff Mason. 'Sheriff Mason, would you say that Mr. Dunn here is a man of his word?'

'Absolutely,' replied the sheriff. 'I have no doubt about it.'

The lawman turned back toward Ben. 'In that case, I'll be on my way. Please don't plan to leave until I have a chance to serve this warrant.'

'I can't do that,' protested Ben. 'I have a business to attend to in town. Besides, it would be extremely inappropriate for me to stay here alone with my fiancée.'

'Well, then you'll need to be escorted back to town. Come with me and we'll talk this out with the sheriff.'

The two men walked out to Sheriff Mason. 'Sheriff Mason, I need you to stay here and keep an eye on the house. I'll go back to town and send a deputy out to relieve you. If Mr. Dunn is ready to go back to town now, he can come with me, otherwise he'll need to come in with you once the deputy arrives.'

'I'll wait for the deputy,' replied Ben.

'Fair enough,' replied the marshal as he mounted his horse. 'I'll send a deputy as soon as I get to town.' The lawman turned his horse toward town and headed down the road.

No sooner was he out of sight, Sarah burst out of the house and ran toward the sheriff. 'Mac is no thief and you know it, he didn't steal anyone's cattle,' she cried out.

'Now calm down, Sarah. I'm not the one saying he

91

is.' Suddenly, Sheriff Mason realized what Sarah had just said. 'Say, wait a minute here. How in blazes did you know Mac was being charged with stealing cattle?'

'It's a small town, sheriff, you know that,' interjected Ben.

'It ain't *that* small,' replied Mason.

'Just the same, we know,' said Sarah.

'Does Mac know and is he here?' questioned Sheriff Mason with renewed concern.

'No, Mac doesn't know, and no, he's not here. I gave you my word on that,' replied Ben.

'Well then, can I get off this horse and get out of the sun?' asked the sheriff.

'Why, of course,' replied Sarah. 'I'd invite you in, but under the circumstances. . . .'

'That's quite all right,' replied the sheriff as he dismounted. 'I have to stay here and keep an eye on things. I hope you understand.'

'Not really,' replied Sarah rudely. 'You do what you have to do and I'll do the same.' She walked back to the house and slammed the front door behind her.

Ben stayed behind to talk with the sheriff. 'Listen Joe, I understand you're only doing your job. You'll have to forgive Sarah. This is her brother being accused here. I need to get back to my office. When your deputy comes to replace you, don't leave without me.'

'I'll make sure of that,' replied the sheriff.

He moved into the shade of a nearby pine tree as Ben walked back toward the house.

As Ben walked in, he found Sarah sitting on the edge of a chair with her head in her hands. She looked up at Ben as he walked in the door. 'What happens now?' she wondered out loud. 'I hope Jason finds Mac, but then what? Will they come back here? If he does he'll be arrested. If Mac is guilty, he won't come back. Where will he go? What will he do? Will Jason stay with him? I don't know what to think!' Sarah was beside herself and once again she began to cry.

Ben did his best to console her. 'Sarah, we don't have the answers to these questions. We just need to believe that Jason will find him and warn him. That's all we can hope for. After that, it's up to Mac to decide what he wants to do. It's not in our hands. All we can do is stay strong. There are things that need to be taken care of here. The hired hands will watch over the place for the next few days. After that, we'll just have to wait and see what happens. We'll keep things going here as long as we have to. Mac can take care of himself, whatever he decides to do.'

'How are we going to run this place? We both have jobs in town.' She stood up and began to pace the room. 'We can't be in both places!'

Ben replied. 'Sarah, if Mac doesn't return, let's

hope Jason has enough sense to distance himself and return back here. He'll have to help run the place. If that doesn't happen, I'll hire another hand to help out around here until we get a better picture of what we're up against. For now, the best thing we can do is not panic.'

Sarah began to calm down. Ben had a way of doing that to her. He was her rock and that was one of the things she loved about him. 'What about for now?' she asked.

'For now, I need to head back to town,' replied Ben. 'I plan to do that when Joe's deputy shows up. Do you want to go back as well?'

'No,' Sarah replied. 'I'll stay here for a few days. The hired hands still need to eat. And like you said, let's hope Jason has enough sense to come back. I'll need to be away from the office for a few days.'

'That sounds like a good plan, Sarah. I'll come out as often as I can.' Ben caught Sarah as she paced past him and gave her a reassuring hug. 'I love you, Sarah McKinney.'

'I love you too, Ben Dunn.' Sarah held him close for a long minute.

The deputy had arrived. Sheriff Mason and Ben began a very long and quiet ride back to town. About a mile before they reached Fort Scott they met Marshal Danner on the road.

'Sheriff Mason. I appreciate all the help you've given me. I'm on my way to Mound City. I'm hoping I can intercept Mr. Shepard along the way. He won't be expecting the warrant so I'll have the element of surprise on my side. If he should happen to get by me, it'll be up to your deputy stationed at the ranch to make the arrest.'

'All my deputies understand their duties,' replied Mason.

'Very good,' replied Danner. 'I'm on my way.' He passed by and continued toward Mound City. Marshal Danner was proving himself to be a very impatient man. Unaware of the old road, he took the new road, never suspecting he was on a wild goose chase.

'He should have just waited it out here,' grumbled Mason as the two men rode on. 'Why hell, all he has is a name. He doesn't even know who he's looking for.'

CHAPTER 6

ON THE RUN

Jason made good time along the old road to Mound City.

It was on the second day, as the sun sank low on the horizon, when he first spotted him. Jason had decided to scout out a place to make camp for the night and was just about to turn off the trail when he noticed a lone rider heading toward him. He was leading a young bull tethered on the end of a rope. Jason wondered if this might be Mac. His suspicion was confirmed when he recognized the rider's voice as he called out for permission to pass. Jason was thankful he hadn't turned off the trail yet.

'Permission denied,' he replied. 'Come closer and

let me get a look at you.' Mac rode closer until they were close enough to recognize each other. Mac took a double take before a wide smile of recognition crossed his face. He dismounted as he called out. 'Jason, never in my wildest dreams would I have expected to meet you here. What in the hell are you doing in this part of the country? I thought you were in Texas?'

Jason dismounted and the two hugged. Mac put his hands on Jason's shoulders and held him at arm's length as he looked him up and down. 'You've grown. You're looking more like a man and less like a kid, that's for sure. Where on earth are you heading?'

Jason looked Mac in the eye, but didn't answer the question. 'Let's make camp. I'll tell you then.'

They found their spot, bedded their horses down for the night, kindled a fire and cooked up a hearty meal.

After they had eaten and caught each other up with small talk, Mac brought up the question again. 'So tell me, where are you heading?'

Jason thoughtfully poked at the fire with a stick. He took the glowing end and tapped it on a rock, creating a few sparks that quickly got caught up with the smoke and disappeared out of sight. Without removing his gaze from the burning embers, he answered. 'I came to find you.' Jason turned his head toward Mac. 'There's trouble. You can't go back home.'

Mac was a bit puzzled. 'What are you talking about, I can't go back home? What kind of trouble? I'm not understanding. . . .'

Mac's face showed dim in the firelight, but Jason could see he was truly confused. 'You've been found out,' replied Jason. 'I'm not sure how. Ben came out to the ranch to warn you, but you were already gone. He said there was a marshal in Fort Scott with a warrant for your arrest . . . for rustling cattle. They could hang you for that.'

Mac didn't readily reply. He just stared at the fire, thinking. Finally, he let it out. 'Shit, it was a damn foolish and stupid thing to do. I knew it at the time, but I was desperate. I didn't know how else to raise the money I needed to keep the ranch. I knew it was wrong when I did it. I could feel it in my bones, but like a damn fool I ignored it. And here's something else. I knew someone was on to me. I just didn't want to believe it.'

'How did you know it?' asked Jason.

'Someone sent me a note. They left it on my front doorstep. It was signed by someone named Micah. I don't know of anyone named Micah. I'm thinking Miles Hanley put it there to unnerve me. It worked to a degree.' He chuckled as he commented. 'Miles was pretty pissed that night, wasn't he?' The smile quickly left his face. He stopped talking and stared blankly at the fire.

Sitting silently, he considered his options. Eventually, he got up and threw another log on the dimming fire, then asked Jason the question that was most on his mind. 'So what about you? Are they after you as well?'

'I don't think so. My name didn't come up, only yours,' replied Jason.

Mac was happy to hear that bit of good news. 'Well that relieves me some. I'm afraid I need to rely on you more than ever now.'

'I'm with you. Where do we go from here?' inquired Jason.

'Well, whatever I decide to do, we're not doing it together. This is my problem and I'm not going to drag you into it any more than you already are. I need to figure out a plan, but as for you, I really need you to go back to the ranch. You need to run things for me until . . . well . . . until . . .' Mac's words suddenly trailed off. '. . . I don't know. That's something I still need to figure out.' Once again Mac went silent as he became lost in his thoughts. The realization that he could very well end up losing the ranch anyhow, as well as his freedom and possibly his very life, was beginning to sink in.

Jason kept quiet. He was lost in his *own* thoughts. Running Mac's ranch wasn't really what he wanted to do with his life, but how could he refuse. He had worked for Mac and Miles Hanley at the XO and had a pretty good idea of how things went. Sarah was taking care of Mac's paperwork, so that was good. He could probably make a go of it if Mac's hired hands were any good. Even though Mac wasn't quite ready to admit it, he was in a fix and there seemed to be no way around it. He was now a wanted man and in all likelihood would never make it back to the ranch. That thought was Jason's last as he settled in for the night. Mac hugged the fire a while longer. He had decisions to make.

Before the morning sun had crested the horizon, Mac was up. He hadn't slept much. Decisions had been made and now he ate a quick breakfast and saddled up. Jason poked at his grub. He wasn't in a hurry and found it hard to focus on what the new day was about to bring his way. He gave Mac what supplies he had as well as all the money he was carrying.

'You be sure Sarah pays you back from out of my account,' ordered Mac.

He handed Jason a piece of neatly folded paper. 'Last-minute instructions to Sarah. Make sure she gets it. As for you, if I need anything, I'll send a telegram signed Tex.' Mac gave Jason one last hug and then mounted up. He reached out his hand to Jason one last time. 'Take care of the ranch, son, and Sarah too.' They shook and Mac pulled away.

'Where are you heading?' asked Jason.

'Best you don't know,' replied Mac. Abruptly, he kicked his horse into a run, purposely deciding not to look back. Truth be told, he wasn't quite sure what direction to go. Finally, he pointed the gelding's nose west, determined to go as far as the trail would take him, and then head south to Mexico. Other than that, he had no real plan.

Jason poured a cup of coffee and sat down near the fire. He drank it slowly as he pondered the events of the past year, especially the last twenty-four hours. *At this rate, he thought, I'm going to be an old man before I turn seventeen.* He cursed and threw the dregs from his cup into the fire. *Shit! I don't want this; all this responsibility. It's too soon; too damned soon.*

Resigned to his fate, he cleared the camp, grabbed up the new bull's tether and headed down the road.

Marshal Danner stayed on the new trail all the way into Mound City, with nothing more than a vague description from Sheriff Mason and the fact that it would be someone leading a young bull. His plan, if he met up with Mac, was to make small talk to get his name. When he had that confirmed, he would make the arrest. Danner, not finding what he was looking for, never got the chance.

Once in Mound City, Danner began to ask around

until he was given the name of a rancher who might have sold Mac the bull. It was indeed, but the rancher had sold Mac the bull three days earlier. When Danner heard this news he figured there was no way to catch up to him. He wondered how he could have missed him along the trail. Mac was probably back at the ranch by now, and hopefully in jail. Danner decided to spend the night in Mound City and head back to Fort Scott in the morning.

As he rode down Main Street he noticed the local saloon, called the Maverick, was open for business. He hadn't had a drink in a week and since no one would know him in this little hole-in-the-wall town, he decided to stop in and have a shot or two.

Danner hid his badge and walked in the front door of the Maverick and headed straight for the bar.

'What'll it be?' asked the bartender.

'Whiskey will do,' replied Danner. His mouth began to water in anticipation as the bartender poured his glass right up to the rim.

No sooner was the glass full, Danner downed it. 'I'll have another,' he requested with eager anticipation.

The bartender filled the glass again and Danner downed it immediately. 'Why don't you just leave the bottle,' requested Danner as he laid his money on the bar.'

'You look like a mighty thirsty man,' noted the bartender. 'Here you go.'

The bartender left the bottle and took the money.

Danner nursed the next few drinks and was about to finish off the bottle when a young cowboy walked up to his table. 'I couldn't help but notice you from across the room,' said the young man. 'I think I know you. Weren't you in Kansas City a few months back? Seems I recall you gettin' drunk and into one hell of a fight over one thing or another.'

'Wasn't me, kid,' replied Danner. 'Why don't you just move along?'

'No, no. I remember that fight clear as day. You almost beat that poor man to death. You got yourself arrested. I know that for a fact. Yup, I'm sure it was you.'

Danner had heard enough. If the kid wasn't going to shut up on his own, he would help him out some. He stood up and grabbed the kid by the shirt with his left hand and let loose a powerful right to the side of the head. The punch would have put down most men, but the kid was scrappy and he came back at Danner with a hard right of his own, knocking Danner off balance.

Danner grabbed a chair and swung it at the kid, missing him and crashing it into the bar. The chair shattered into pieces and scattered across the room. This prompted two others to get involved, but Danner was having no part of it. He thrashed out like a wild man. It was turning into quite a ruckus when a

103

shot rang out above the noise. It stopped most every-one in their tracks except for Danner, who pulled his gun even though he had no real target in sight.

'Drop that weapon before I drop you,' shouted out the sheriff as he leveled his sights on to Danner.

Danner was drunk and not thinking clearly. He pointed his gun at the sheriff, who wasted little time in pulling the trigger, hitting Danner in the shoulder, spinning him around and causing him to drop his weapon.

The sheriff picked up Danner's gun and asked one of the men still in the saloon to run ahead and let Doc Green know there was a patient coming his way. He motioned with the barrel of his gun for Danner to move toward the door. He marched his new pris-oner over to the doctor's office. 'That was a damn fool thing to do, mister. You're lucky I didn't kill you,' commented the sheriff as they walked down the street. Once they arrived at Doc Green's office the sheriff was greeted with friendly banter. 'Sheriff Cutler, I'm so glad you only wound the men you shoot. I'm sure I appreciate your business more than the undertaker does. Not too often they walk in on their own, though.'

'Sometimes they get lucky,' replied Cutler.

As Doc Green worked on patching up Danner's shoulder, Sheriff Cutler began to question him.

'What's your name?' he asked.

'None of your business,' replied Danner as the doctor worked at digging the bullet out of his shoulder. Danner winced, but held back on yelling out.

'I'll find out soon enough,' answered the sheriff. 'Once I get you situated in your new room, compliments of Mound City.'

It was an easy fix for the Doc. And once he finished the patchwork, the sheriff escorted Danner to the jailhouse and ordered him to empty his pockets on to the desk before he put him into his cell. Danner complied and when he threw down his badge the sheriff took notice. 'Well, well. What have we here?' He picked up the badge for a closer look. 'US Marshal?' he questioned.

'That's right. I'm on official business,' replied Danner. 'I'm working with Sheriff Joe Mason in Fort Scott.'

Sheriff Cutler tossed the badge back down on to the desk and escorted Danner into an empty cell. Danner sat down on the cot as the sheriff closed the cell door and locked it. 'Well for now, you're officially my prisoner.'

'So what's your name and just what might your official business be?' asked the sheriff.

'I'm Marshal Dan Danner and I'm here to serve a warrant. The paperwork is on your desk,' Danner motioned toward the personal belongings he had just unloaded.

Sheriff Cutler unfolded the papers and began to read them. 'This here says your man is in Fort Scott. What are you doing here in Mound City?'

'He was here on business. I tried to head him off, but I was too late.'

The sheriff didn't reply. He picked up the badge and paperwork, walked out the door and headed straight for the telegraph office where he sent out a few inquiries about US Marshal Dan Danner.

He knew something was up and he wanted some answers. This marshal was drunk on duty and causing quite a ruckus to boot. This left a bad taste in Cutler's mouth and he hoped to find out why. The answer arrived within a couple of hours. What he found out was unsettling to say the least. It seems Marshal Dan Danner had never been heard of. As far as Sheriff Cutler could figure out, Danner wasn't a US Marshal, only impersonating one. He knew Sheriff Mason and decided to send him a telegram, which he did. He then walked back to his office.

As he walked through the doorway, he noticed that Danner was asleep on his cot. 'Hey you, wake up,' he called out.

Danner opened his eyes, but didn't move much.

The sheriff stepped up to the bars. 'I made a few inquiries and it turns out nobody seems to know you. You're not a US Marshal and as far as I can tell, I seriously doubt if you ever have been. In fact, I'm wondering if Dan Danner is even your real name. What do you have to say about it?'

'I got nothin' to say,' replied Danner.

'Seems the charges against you are adding up. Drunk and disorderly and now impersonating a US Marshal. What else am I going to find? Why are you after Mac Shepard? Paperwork says cattle rustling. Is that a fact? Who wrote out this paperwork and who hired you?'

'You ask a hell of a lot of questions,' stated Danner as he sat up, trying to reposition his sore shoulder.

'And you don't seem to have any of the answers,' replied the sheriff. 'You've got a lot of explaining to do, if not to me, then to someone further up the line.'

Danner lay back down on the cot. 'Like I said, I got nothin' to say.'

'Your choice,' replied Cutler as he walked back over to his desk and sat down. He took Danner's personal belongings and shoved them into one of the drawers of his desk. As he did, he noticed a small slip of paper that had previously gone unnoticed. He unfolded it to find a name written on it. Miles Hanley XO.

The sheriff called out to Danner. 'Who's Miles Hanley?'

Danner got up off the cot and stood in front of the bars. 'Where did you hear that name?' he questioned.

107

'Didn't hear it, I read it. It's out of your pocket.' The sheriff held up the slip of paper and waved it as if flaunting it in Danner's face.

'It's nothin', get the hell out of my personal papers,' shouted Danner.

'Well now, seems *nothin'* was enough to get you off that cot and yellin'. That in itself seems to make it somethin', not nothin', don't you think? XO, now that sounds like maybe it could be a brand. So maybe I'll just have to check this out. My investigation into who you are is just beginning, Mr. Dan Danner, if that's your real name. I'll get to the bottom of it with or without your help. Until then, you're mine. I hope you enjoy your stay.' With that, Sheriff Cutler got up from his chair and headed back out the door. He had more telegrams to send.

Cutler sent out telegrams to towns in all directions hoping at least one sheriff would be able to shed some light on this mystery. Who is Dan Danner? Who is Mac Shepard? Who is Miles Hanley XO? Who was behind all this and why?

When Sheriff Mason received the second telegram from Sheriff Cutler indicating that Marshal Danner might be an impostor, he decided to take a trip to Mound City and pay the sheriff a personal visit. He replied that he had information and that he would be making the trip to see him. Sheriff Mason loaded up his gear and rode out to the Shepard ranch, where he met up with his deputy who was on duty watching for Mac to return from Mound City. 'No sense hanging around here. I have word that Marshal Danner may not be who he says he is, so even if Mac does show up, we may not have cause to arrest him. I'm on my way to Mound City to try and make sense of this whole affair. I'll be back within the week.' he told the deputy. 'Keep a good eye on things while I'm gone.' He then went up to the house to talk with Sarah.

Mason knew Sarah was upset with him, so he tried to be as delicate as possible. He knocked and she answered the door. When she opened it, Mason pulled off his hat. 'Sarah, ma'am, I just want to let you know that I'm sending my deputy home. There seems to be some question about this whole thing about Mac.' He went on. 'I'm on my way to Mound City to try and get to the bottom of it all. When Mac shows up, please have him stick around and I'll fill him in when I get back.'

Sarah was still unhappy about the whole situation, but thanked him for his professionalism. Mason went back to his horse and continued on to Mound City by way of the new road. It was faster.

Sheriff Mason made it to Mound City in a little over two days. It was early morning when he left his horse at the livery and walked over to the sheriff's office. The door was open so he walked in. Sheriff Cutler was working at his desk, but looked up when Mason walked through the door. 'Joe, how the heck are you?' asked Cutler as he stood to shake hands.

'I'm doing well,' replied Mason. 'There's always something coming up to keep the job interesting.'

'Well isn't that the truth,' answered Cutler. 'In fact I got one here that I think will give us both a run for our money.' Sheriff Cutler pointed over to the cell where Dan Danner was standing at the bars.

Hopeful, Danner greeted Sheriff Mason with a wide smile. 'Please tell the sheriff here what's going on and get me out of this cage.'

'Sheriff Cutler and I need to talk first, then we'll decide on what to do with you,' replied Sheriff Mason.

'Why don't we step outside, Joe. Where we can talk more openly,' suggested Cutler.

The two men went outside and walked down the boardwalk as Sheriff Mason filled in Sheriff Cutler on what he knew.

'He came into my office with paperwork and a badge,' said Mason. 'It all looked in order to me. Said he was after Mac Shepard for rustlin' cattle.'

'I got that part,' replied Cutler. 'But I made some inquiries to a couple of judges I know, who did a little checking of their own. Seems Dan Danner has never

110

been a US Marshal, so I don't really understand why he's pretending to be one, and why he's after Mac Shepard? Not only that. Where does Miles Hanley, XO, fit into all of this?'

'Miles Hanley is a ranch owner down around the Fort Scott area. His brand is the XO. . . .'

'Ah-ha,' interrupted Cutler. 'I thought the XO might have been a brand.'

Mason continued. 'Here's the thing about Miles Hanley. He swears Mac is a cattle thief. Says he almost caught him red-handed. Says Mac loaded the cattle on to a train, but the train was long gone with the cattle when he confronted Mac, who was paying off two men. His son was with him. He told Miles that the two men had kidnapped his son and he was just paying off the ransom. I'll admit it sounds a little fishy, but there's no hard evidence to dispute the claim, so there's not much I can do.'

The two men stopped and sat on an empty bench in front of the general store. Sheriff Cutler rolled a smoke and lit up. Smoke from the quirly rolled from under the brim of his hat as he let it hang from his lips. He leaned forward with his forearms propped against his legs as if in thought. 'I'm still not real sure why Dan Danner is involved in this,' Cutler admitted.

'I might have your answer,' replied Mason. 'The morning after the *alleged* cattle theft, Miles and I got into an argument over the incident. He accused me of not doing enough and that he was going to take matters into his own hands. I cautioned him against it, but at the time, I didn't think he was serious. But now, I'm not so sure.'

'You think Dan Danner might be working for Miles Hanley?' questioned Cutler.

'I think that might be the case,' replied Mason. 'But what I don't know is if Miles believes Danner is for real. If he doesn't know it, that's one thing. If he hired Danner to impersonate a US Marshal, well, that's a whole different kettle of fish.'

'I agree,' answered Cutler as he took the last drag from his smoke and flicked the butt into the street. 'How do you think we should go about getting Danner to fess up?'

'I think we just need to tell him we know he's working for Miles Hanley. Hopefully he'll admit to it and tell us what we want to know. If not, maybe I can trip up Miles, and get him to spill what he knows when I talk to him about this,' replied Mason. 'Here's what we'll do. When we go back, you tell him we contacted Miles, who believes Danner is a bona fide US Marshal, and we plan to throw the book at Danner for impersonating a US Marshal. I'll then play it down and try to bait him to tell me the truth. He knows me some and hopefully trusts me. I did tell him I'd see what I could do to get him out.'

'Sounds like a plan,' replied Cutler. 'Let's give it

an hour or two. We need Danner to think we actually sent the telegram. How about we get some lunch?'

After a leisurely lunch, Cutler and Mason entered Cutler's office. Danner stood and stepped up to the bars. 'Well?'

'Well what?' questioned Cutler.

'Well, when am I getting out of here?' Danner challenged.

Cutler started in on Danner. 'As far as I'm concerned, Danner, I'm throwing away the key on you.' He walked up to the bars as Mason took a seat at his desk to watch the show.

Cutler continued with his concocted story. 'We sent an urgent telegram to Miles Hanley this morning. He got back to us in short order. Says he had made inquiries to the Attorney General's office and thought you were a real US Marshal who had been sent to bring Mac Shepard to justice. He's as surprised as we are that you're an impostor.'

'That makes no sense,' replied Danner. He grabbed the bars and put his face up close. 'If I was an impostor, don't you think the Attorney General would have said so, and why in tarnation would I be after Mac Shepard? There's no reason for it. Why you can't get someone to verify the fact that I'm a bona fide US Marshal is beyond me.'

'Because you're not. Miles Hanley hired you to

impersonate a US Marshal,' retorted Cutler.

'Bullshit,' replied Danner angrily. He reached through the bars and pointed a finger at Cutler. 'You don't know what you're talking about.'

Sheriff Mason figured it was his turn to step in. He got up from his chair and walked over to the cell. 'Mr. Danner, let me tell you what we know.'

Sheriff Cutler took the cue and moved back to his desk.

Sheriff Mason continued. 'Dan, the US Marshal's office isn't going to abandon one of their own. They know who's on their payroll, and they know you're not. As far as they're concerned, you're an impostor.'

Danner continued to listen quietly to what Sheriff Mason had to say.

Mason went on. 'We also know that you're involved with Miles Hanley in some way. What we don't know is how. Does he think you're a real US Marshal, or did he hire you to play the part? If he thinks you're for real, he's off the hook and you take the full amount of charges that come against you. On the other hand, if he hired you to impersonate a US Marshal, he's charged as well.'

'And how does that help me?' asked Danner.

'Listen, Sheriff Cutler wants to throw the book at you. I, on the other hand, am willing to see about getting you a more lenient sentence, if you cooperate with us, that is. I like you, Dan. You seem like a nice kid. I'd hate to see you rot in a federal prison for the rest of your life, especially because you thought keeping your mouth shut about Hanley was the noble thing to do. You rotting in prison and Miles Hanley enjoying the rest of his life in freedom just doesn't seem fair to me. So like I said, if you cooperate with me, I'll do everything I possibly can to get you out of this mess with the least amount of pain. What do you say?'

Danner took a deep breath. He was thinking hard.

From the back of the room Sheriff Cutler shouted out. 'Don't be makin' no deals with him, Mason. I want to see that little bastard rot in prison for the rest of his life.'

Sheriff Mason raised his eyebrows at Danner as if to say, *He's serious, but I've got your back.*

Danner really didn't like the idea of spending the rest of his life in prison. If spilling the beans to Sheriff Mason would help him out, he was ready to do it. 'Do you really think you can help me?'

'I told you I'd do whatever I could, but you've got to level with me,' replied Mason.

'OK, fine,' Danner opened up and told Mason all the details. 'Miles Hanley and I have worked on other 'land projects' in the past. He's after Mac Shepard's place and needs him out of the way. He apparently tried to do it through you, but the lack of evidence held you back. He then went to the

115

Attorney General's office who told him the same thing. He needed hard evidence. He hired me, hoping that I could somehow smoke him out and get a confession from him. I guess that's no longer in the cards, is it?'

Mason questioned Danner. 'Do you mean to tell me this is all about land and not about cattle?'

'Oh no,' replied Danner. 'It is about cattle. Miles firmly believes Mac Shepard is guilty of cattle rustling. He just needs to prove it. Once he legally gets Shepard out of the way, he'll have a chance at getting his hands on his ranch.'

'So did Miles hire you to impersonate a US Marshal?' asked Mason.

'No, he hired me to get proof. A confession out of Mac would have done the trick. The US Marshal idea was my own. My plan was to arrest him and bring him to you . . . with his confession.'

'Considering how you were planning to go about getting it, his confession would have been worthless. You would have been better off taking him to the town preacher, not me,' replied Mason.

'Well in any case, that's about the extent of it. You're not going to go back on your word now, are you?' Danner was getting worried he'd been had.

'I gave you my word,' replied Mason. 'I'll do what I can.'

Mason stepped away from the bars and signaled

for Cutler to step outside.

'Well I'll be damned,' stated Cutler. 'I'm genuinely impressed. You got what we needed.'

'We got it,' replied Mason. 'We were good, weren't we?'

'So Danner is an impostor hired by Miles Hanley, not only to prove Mac Shepard's guilt, but to get his hands on his ranch as well. The shit just keeps getting deeper, doesn't it?' Cutler commented.

Mason thoughtfully replied. 'The good thing for Miles is that you can't arrest a man for covetousness. The fact that he didn't know Danner was going to pass himself off as a US Marshal saved his bacon.'

'Now what?' questioned Cutler.

'I need to head back to Fort Scott and have a talk with Miles Hanley. I'll also need to let Mac and his kin know what's going on. Neither conversation is one I'm looking forward to. I'll also keep my word to Danner. Once he's charged, I'll send a telegram to the prosecutor and let him know he cooperated with our investigation.'

The two men spent the rest of the day taking it easy and swapping stories. The following morning Sheriff Joe Mason headed back to Fort Scott.

As Sheriff Mason drew close to Mac Shepard's ranch, he stopped and took in a deep breath. His stomach was unsettled. It was good news for Mac, but Mason still didn't like the idea of having to explain the whole situation. As Mason came up to the gate he noticed Ben's horse tied to the rail. He tied his and went up to the door. Ben saw him coming and he and Sarah stepped out to greet him. Jason stayed out of sight as he wasn't sure what to expect.

'Good afternoon, Ben, Sarah. Is Mac here? I have good news for him, and you.'

'Mac isn't here right now,' replied Sarah. 'What's your news?'

Sheriff Mason was hesitant to tell anyone other than Mac, but under the circumstances, he thought it might be best to let it out and not wait for Mac. He really didn't want to have to do this twice. So he went ahead. 'As I'm sure you know, I've been in Mound City. Turns out Dan Danner isn't a US Marshal after all. He's an imposter. So Mac has nothing to worry about. There are no charges being leveled against him.'

'I'm not sure I'm understanding,' replied Ben. 'If Danner wasn't a marshal, why was he pretending to be one, and why was he after Mac for rustling cattle?'

'I'm not at liberty to say,' replied Sheriff Mason rather hesitantly. 'If Mac were here. . . .'

'Well, Mac isn't here,' interrupted Sarah angrily. 'Mac never came home from his trip to Mound City. He apparently heard a US Marshal was after him and he went into hiding.'

'Went into hiding?' questioned Mason. 'Why would he do that if he were innocent?'

'You'd run too if you were about to be lynched,' added Ben. 'You've pretty much just confirmed that someone wants Mac out of the way bad enough to pretend to be a US Marshal and arrest him. Then what, shoot him or lynch him? There are those who believe Mac rustled cattle and a lynching wouldn't be out of the realm of possibilities, you know.'

'Well, I'll agree with you there, Ben. I hope he shows back up. There won't be a lynching on my watch. I give you my word. I'm truly sorry for the trouble this has caused you.'

'We have a good idea who's behind this, sheriff. When you see Miles, you tell him to back off. He may be my uncle, but Sarah is soon to be my wife, and Mac is her brother. If he wants to talk about this like an adult, he knows where to find me.'

'Assuming Miles is involved in this, I'll let him know,' replied Mason as he tipped his hat and took his leave.

Sheriff Mason was glad to have that conversation behind him. Now on to Miles Hanley, but first a hot meal in Fort Scott was on his mind. He *really* wasn't looking forward to the conversation he would have with Miles and decided to put it off for now. Tomorrow would be another day.

Call it bad luck, or maybe fate. Whatever it was,

Sheriff Mason rode right into it as he reached Fort Scott. He stepped off his horse in front of his office just as Miles Hanley was walking up the boardwalk. *Damn*, thought Mason when he saw Miles. *I really didn't want to do this now, but I might as well get it over with.*

'Good afternoon, Miles. How are you today?'

'I'm just fine,' replied Miles as he continued to walk on by.

With the greetings out of the way, Mason called out. 'Say Miles, do you have a minute? I need to talk with you.'

'Not now,' Miles replied. 'I'm in a bit of a hurry.'

Mason wasn't about to take no for an answer. 'Well, then just slow yourself down and step into my office. . . . Now! We need to talk.'

Miles could see that Sheriff Mason was upset, so he did as he was told and the two men stepped into the lawman's office. One of his deputies was at the desk and Mason asked him to leave. 'Have a seat, Miles,' suggested Mason as he pointed to a chair across from his desk. Miles sat down as Sheriff Mason stood in front of him and rested his butt against the edge of the desk. The tactic clearly put Sheriff Mason in a superior position of authority. 'Do you have any idea where I've been for the past few days, or what the hell I've been doing?' he asked. His voice betrayed his frustration.

120

'No, can't say as I do,' replied Miles.

'Does the name Dan Danner ring any bells in that fool head of yours?' questioned Mason.

Miles kept quiet as he thought about how he wanted to answer the question. 'I've heard of him.'

'HEARD OF HIM! Damn right you've heard of him. YOU HIRED HIM!' yelled Mason. 'Did you know he was arrested in Mound City for impersonating a United States Marshal? And did you also know that he implicated you in a plot to remove Mac Shepard from his ranch?' Sheriff Mason was fuming and Miles suddenly found himself to be in a very uncomfortable position.

'OK, yes, I did hire him,' answered Miles. 'I hired Dan Danner to smoke Mac out. I realized the only evidence I would ever have against Mac was his very own confession. I never conspired with Danner to impersonate a US Marshal or anyone else as far as that goes. He was on his own. If he's trying to say I had anything to do with that, I'll flatly deny it to my last breath.'

Mason didn't let up. 'And what do you have to say about Danner's accusation that getting a confession from Mac was not the sole reason for you hiring him? That in fact, the reason you wanted to get Mac out of the picture was part of a bigger plan to take over his ranch? Danner admits he has worked with you in the past on your dirty dealings. And the whole damned town has heard the rumors of how you acquired a portion of the XO. It sounds to me like those stories may in fact be true.'

Miles couldn't tolerate sitting under the shadow of Sheriff Mason's towering figure any longer. He pushed back his chair, stood up and moved several feet away from the lawman. 'Danner is a liar. This has nothing to do with the Shepard ranch, only Mac Shepard. He thinks he can run that ranch off the backs of the men he stole cattle from. I'm not about to let him get away with it.'

Sheriff Mason pointed an authoritative finger at Miles. 'And just who the hell made you God Almighty? You're about to wind up in jail, Miles. That's what all of this is getting you. Mac has disappeared. He never returned from Mound City and quite frankly, even though Danner didn't admit to it, I'm wondering if there might not be foul play involved here. You could find yourself charged with being an accomplice to murder.'

'Murder! You've got to be kidding me!' replied Miles, the concern evident in his voice.

Before Mason had a chance to reply, Miles continued. 'Did you say Mac hasn't come home? Well, if he's on the run, wouldn't that be proof enough that he was guilty?'

'All that proves is that he didn't want to be lynched. Why hell, your own nephew did the same thing,' Mason retorted. 'Ben's a well-respected doctor in this town now. He wasn't guilty of anything when he ran from a lynch mob and Mac may not be either. Fact is, you're not hearing a word I'm saying. You could be the one with your neck in a noose, not Mac.'

'Are you arresting me, Joe?' asked Miles.

'No, I'm not. At least not right now. You had better hope Mac shows up, is all I've got to say.'

'Danner isn't a killer. I'm not worried about that,' replied Miles. 'If you're finished, I'll be leaving.'

'I'm done with you for now, Miles. As far as finished goes, I only hope that's the case.'

Miles walked out the door somewhat relieved, but extremely unhappy at the turn of events. Nothing had gone as he had planned.

Sheriff Mason was also relieved to have that conversation behind him. He was still hungry and headed out the door in search of some supper. He stopped short when he realized his horse was still tied to the hitch rail. Supper would have to wait. He had a horse to tend to.

CHAPTER 7

A PLAN OF SORTS

Six long days had passed since Mac had been told by
Jason that there was a US Marshal after him with a
warrant for his arrest. Not knowing who might be on
his trail or how far behind him they were, he kept
moving. Where to, he still wasn't quite sure. He'd
had plenty of time to think things through.
Hopefully he could get far enough away to where he
would never be found. He knew his geography and
had always had a hankerin' to see what South
America was like. Maybe he could make it there and
start over. He would eventually need a way to make
some money. What he had wouldn't last forever and
there was no way to get to his bank account. He
doubted if he would ever make it back to his ranch.

The note he had given Jason for Sarah laid it all out. She was to take care of the ranch, with Jason's help. And when Jason turned twenty-one, it would all go to him.

Everything he had. Everything he had worked for. All of his plans and all of his dreams were gone. In all likelihood, he would never see his family again. All because of a damn fool decision to steal another man's cattle. He kicked himself every time he thought about it. He still had his life, for now. It was the last thing he had worth saving, so he rode on.

When he hit Denver, he reconsidered his plan. His horse was too slow and they were both getting tired, so he sold the horse and most of his gear, bought a train ticket and headed to California. He finally had some sort of an idea of what he wanted to do.

Before he left Denver he sent a telegram to Fort Scott.

It read . . . *Jason, I have a plan. Someday I'll fill you in. Take care.* He signed it 'Tex'.

Jason got the telegram. He was glad to know Mac was getting things figured out. He only wished he could let him know that he was running for nothing. Jason sent a reply, but doubted if 'Tex' would get it.

He didn't.

Mac rode the train for close to a week. It rolled through some of the prettiest country he had ever laid eyes on. Tall fir trees and fertile green valleys.

Rushing rivers, rolling hills and rugged mountains. He had no idea how beautiful and how rugged the land out west could be. There were several times when he thought he would just step off the train and spend the rest of his life right where his foot touched the ground. But Mac was running scared and he had developed a plan over the past week that he hoped would save him from the hangman's noose. It involved getting out of the country, and that meant putting the miles behind him as fast as possible. There was no time for sightseeing other than the brief glimpses of a beautiful land that whizzed by the windows of the train he was on.

For Mac, the ride ended in San Francisco, California. He had put nearly eighteen hundred miles behind him in a little more than two weeks. An impossible feat several years earlier. In San Francisco, he thought about sending a 'Tex' telegram to Jason, but thought better of it considering it might tip off someone in Fort Scott as to his whereabouts. Sarah and Jason would just have to wait and wonder.

From here, Mac's plan was to catch a steamship to Panama. He had heard stories of how men on the east coast used this route to get to the gold fields of California during the height of the gold rush. They took steamships down the east coast to Panama, then went overland to ports on the Pacific side and caught another steamship to California. And from here they made their way to the gold fields. Nowadays these same ships were transporting more cargo than men and he was hoping to get on board one heading south.

He walked down to the docks where several ships were being loaded. They were as busy as the stockyards in Kansas, but here they were moving mostly cargo and only a few people, although he did come across a corral that was used for holding cattle, but it was empty. During the war, he had heard about cattle being brought in from other countries, but couldn't imagine why.

He stood leaning against the fence with a boot on the bottom rail. He could smell the remains of recent activity through the salt air. It reminded him of home. It was the only familiar thing he had found since he left Fort Scott. He was already beginning to miss it.

'Hey, you there, leaning up against the fence,' called out a booming voice. 'You want to earn a couple dollars? I unloaded a hundred head yesterday. I can usually find someone around here to do some work for me. Today just might be your lucky day, as long as you can stand the smell of cattle shit.'

Mac looked the man over before he answered. He was big in the belly and didn't look like he was much good at any real physical labor. He chewed tobacco. As Mac was sizing him up, he spit; it didn't all make it past his full beard. He wiped his mouth with the sleeve of his shirt.

'Follow me,' he continued, not waiting for an answer. 'My name's Captain Pappy and this here's my ship. I call her Annabelle.' The two men walked down the dock and up the wide gangplank that entered an opening in the side toward the stern. Two large hatches on the deck were open which let in plenty of daylight. The pungent smell of cattle waste was almost overpowering.

'I need her shoveled out and hosed down in less than two days, so I can load her with cargo,' remarked Pappy.

Mac noticed two other men with shovels already working. 'Where's the cargo heading?' he asked.

'Hawaii,' replied Pappy.

'Hawaii, not Panama?' questioned Mac.

'Annabelle goes to Hawaii and back. That's it. I'm asking you to shovel shit. Why does it matter where I'm headin'?' inquired Pappy.

Mac had to make a quick decision that would once again change his plan, but it would get him out of the country and that's what he was after. 'I'll tell you what, Pappy. I'll help clean this up for nothing more than a small space on your ship from here to Hawaii.'

'No deal,' replied Pappy. 'If you ride on my ship, you work all the way. You shovel shit here. You help load the cargo, and once we're underway, you shovel coal until we get there, and then you help unload. I'll feed you and give you a place to sleep. See those two boys workin', they're full-time crew members. They're good men, but they need help. It'll take all three of you working shifts once we're underway. That's the deal, OK?'

Mac decided to take Pappy up on the offer. 'You got a deal,' he replied. 'Where do I get a shovel?'

Pappy spit, wiped his beard on the sleeve of his dirty shirt and shook hands with Mac. 'That's what I like to hear. Hang what gear you have on the bulkhead where that shovel hangs. That'll be yours for the duration.' Pappy pointed across the room. 'One more thing. If you turn out to be worthless, these two may just throw you overboard.' Pappy let out a laugh. He apparently thought that was pretty funny. Mac didn't see the humor.

Trading his gear, which was nothing more than his saddlebags, for the shovel, he went to work. The other two men kept to themselves talking periodically in a language Mac didn't understand. They were hard workers and it was all Mac could do to keep up.

After two days of hard labor shoveling and hosing down the cargo hold it was ready to be loaded up. The three men on board and another couple from the dock spent a full day filling the hold with crates and sacks of assorted merchandise, and the coal bin with a fresh supply of fuel. After a hard three days they were underway. Mac felt a sense of relief once they pulled away from the dock. The two men he was working with were nice enough. One spoke some broken English, so between the three of them they were able to communicate well enough to get by. The weather was in their favor and Pappy turned out to be a likable fellow. Once they made it to Hawaii, Pappy kept him on long enough to unload the cargo and then load it up again with cargo going back to San Francisco. Once that was done Pappy paid him along with a ten-dollar bonus. Mac decided to take a couple of days to enjoy the change of climate and ask around about finding some work. It turned out there were cattle ranches in Hawaii. He easily found work at one of the bigger spreads on the island.

CHAPTER 8

THE SHEPARD RANCH

It had been over a month since Mac had sent the telegraph to Jason. Miles Hanley was unaware of the contact and as far as anyone other than Jason, Sarah and Ben was concerned, Mac had dropped off the face of the earth. As the days and weeks passed, Miles was beginning to grow nervous. He didn't think Dan Danner was capable of foul play, but with no sign of Mac, he was beginning to wonder if Danner hadn't done him in and buried the body somewhere. Danner had already gone to trial and been found guilty of impersonating a US Marshal, on more than one occasion in fact. He was sentenced to the new prison in Petersburg. There was some short-lived talk of retrying him for murder, but without a body, the evidence needed to prosecute just didn't exist. The talk died down pretty quickly, which was a big relief to Miles, as he could have been tried as an accomplice if they had decided to proceed.

Since the day Danner was arrested, Miles was trying to stay on the good side of Sarah and Jason. It had come out that he had hired Danner to smoke out Mac by getting him to admit to rustling cattle. Even though there was no crime committed on Miles' part, it did put a huge wedge between the XO and the Shepard ranch. Even so, Miles still held out the misguided hope of acquiring the ranch at some point.

Jason was not overly excited about helping Sarah run the Shepard ranch. He still wanted to be on the move. He had recently turned seventeen and his restlessness at times was difficult to subdue, but the hard work, long hours and responsibility kept his wanderlust in check. As the weeks went by, he was beginning to believe that this was his punishment for the part he had played in Mac's cattle-rustling venture.

Whenever possible, Jason would head into town to get a few supplies, and as was his habit, he poked his head into the telegraph office to see if there was anything for him. As usual, the answer was no telegram, but this time there was a postal letter waiting for him.

Jason anxiously took the letter. The upper left corner had one word, Tex. The stamp and cancellation showed the country of Hawaii. As he was looking at the envelope, the clerk asked. 'Who do you know in Hawaii?'

Jason looked up. 'Oh, someone I knew in school,' he replied. 'I haven't heard from him in quite a while.' He anxiously took the letter outside and opened it.

It read . . . *Jason, Hope you are well. Just a note to let you know I'm out of the country and I'm starting over, working cattle for a large outfit here. All is well. Tell Sarah to fill you in on the letter I had you give her when I left, and also tell her I'm sorry I missed the wedding. I wish her and Ben all the best. Maybe someday we'll meet up again, Tex.*

There was no return address, so Jason had no way to contact Mac and let him know about the events that had taken place with Dan Danner. Mac had left everything he loved, his ranch, his family and his country, as he ran to save his very life. His dishonesty had caught up with him and taken away all the things he had worked so hard to build. *Funny how things work out,* thought Jason. He put the letter in his pocket and headed over to Ben's office to see Sarah.

Sarah caught a glimpse of Jason as he entered the office. She flashed him a smile as she finished talking with one of Ben's patients. Jason waited for her to finish. As soon as the patient left the office, she got up and gave Jason a big hug. 'What a surprise to see you here today,' she said. Her smile quickly turned serious as her motherly concern kicked in. 'You're not sick are you?' she questioned.

'No, I'm feeling pretty good today,' he replied with a smile on his face. 'I have a surprise for you.'

'For me? Well, what is it?' she anxiously questioned.

Jason handed her the note. 'It's from Mac,' he quietly stated.

Sarah was slightly stunned to hear the news as she hadn't heard a thing since he left for Mound City several months earlier. 'Mac! Oh, my goodness, are you sure? Where is he?' She called for Ben, who stepped out of his office to find Sarah in a fluster. She and Jason were just stepping outside, as Sarah felt the need for some fresh air. The two sat down on a bench in the shade as Ben walked out the door behind them.

'What's going on?' he asked curiously.

Sarah was smiling as she held up the envelope and waved it in the air. 'Jason has heard from Mac!'

Jason prompted her. 'Well open it up and read it.'

Sarah pulled the note from its envelope and read it out loud. Tears began to roll down her cheeks even though she was a bit confused. 'I'm not understanding? This is signed Tex, not Mac. Are you sure this is from Mac?'

Jason explained to Sarah how he and Mac had decided to use the name Tex as a type of code so others wouldn't know who it was from. Once she understood, the tears resumed. 'I'm so glad he's alive, but this doesn't say where he is except out of the country?'

Jason took the envelope from Sarah and pointed to the stamp. 'All we have to go by is this cancellation stamp that says Hawaii.'

'Hawaii, where's Hawaii?' questioned Sarah.

'I'm not too sure,' replied Jason.

Ben chimed in. 'I know where it is. It's a chain of islands off the coast of California in the middle of the Pacific Ocean. It's a damn long ways from here, that's for sure.'

'But I still don't understand why he's walking away from his ranch. Isn't there some way we can get in touch with him to let him know it was all a big mistake and nobody is after him?' questioned Sarah.

Jason tried to explain. 'Sarah, Mac did a desperate thing when he was about to lose his ranch. He needed money to keep things going. Dan Danner was a fraud, but the charge was true. There's no way to prove it, but I know it to be fact and I'll take that to my grave.'

Sarah was shocked to hear this. It was something that she had always held in the back of her mind, not wanting to consider it as truth, but with this revelation she had no choice but to believe it. 'If Mac is a thief, then I'm ashamed of him,' she bluntly stated.

Jason tried to get Sarah to change her mind. 'He regretted it, he really did, but there was no way to change it. He's paying for his mistake by losing everything he has, short of his life.'

'And so he should,' remarked Sarah. 'He took what didn't belong to him.' She looked back down at the note.

Jason tried to change the subject. 'What's he talking about here?' he questioned as he reached over and pointed at the note. 'Where he says for you to fill me in on the letter he gave you?'

Sarah took a deep breath and composed herself. 'I guess he's not planning to come back, and under the circumstances, I suppose it's for the best. Not too long before he left he signed over the deed to his ranch to me, just in case something happened to him. He wanted to make sure it stayed in the family. I questioned him about it, but all he would tell me was that it was a precaution, against what he wouldn't say. There was one stipulation, and I agreed to it. The stipulation was that when you turned twenty-one, I would sign it over to you. The ranch would be yours.'

Jason's voice betrayed a hint of disbelief. 'You're saying that I'm going to be the owner of Mac's ranch?'

'That's what he wanted,' replied Sarah. 'It seems as if he's resigned himself to the fact that he's not coming back. If he was holding out any hope, he wouldn't have told me to fill you in.'

Jason didn't react. He didn't quite know how. He was sad at the realization that Mac wouldn't be coming home and he wasn't all that happy to hear the news that he would eventually be the owner of the Shepard ranch. It would tie him down for good.

Sarah stood up and handed the note back to Jason. 'This has all been too much for me. I'm going back to work.'

Ben, who had been standing by quietly, asked Sarah if she would rather go home. 'I can handle things around here for the rest of the day,' he added.

'Thank you, Ben, but I need to think about something else right now and work is my distraction. Jason, thank you for bringing me the note and thank you for telling me the truth about Mac.'

'You didn't hear it from me,' he replied as he got up from the bench and headed off to finish his errands.

Ben and Sarah went back inside.

'I can't believe what I just heard. I feel like I just lost my brother,' lamented Sarah.

Ben did his best to console her. 'Don't be so hard on him, Sarah. What he did was wrong and that's a fact, but he's paying for it. He's lost everything he worked for and everyone he loves.'

'That may be true, Ben, but I'll never think of him

in the same light.'

'Well under the circumstances, I wouldn't really expect you to,' replied Ben.

Several weeks had passed and talk of Mac and the ranch had been put aside. Miles was in town to pick up a few supplies when he happened to cross paths with Ben.

'Well hey there, Ben, how have you been? I don't see much of you these days,' commented Miles as he greeted Ben with a hearty handshake.

'You need to get sick more often,' joked Ben. 'How are things at the XO?'

'Couldn't be better,' replied Miles. 'We're getting ready to sell off a couple hundred head. How's that young Jason doing at the Shepard ranch?'

'He's doing well,' replied Ben. 'He has his hands full, that's for sure.'

Miles took this as an opportunity to put in a word to express his interest in buying the ranch, but he played coy. 'Have you had any word from Mac?' he asked.

Ben didn't let on that he had. He felt it was best to keep that quiet. 'Nope, I haven't heard a word.'

'Well, you know, Ben. With Mac being gone so long, I would think there would be some concern about being able to keep up on the mortgage. I assume Sarah has her hands full with running the operation *and* handling the books?'

'Well, you should know, Miles. You've been doing it for years.' Ben could sense something coming from Miles. 'What are you getting at?' he asked.

Miles was not one to beat around the bush, so he came right out and said what was on his mind. 'If Sarah should find the task more than she can handle, I'd be more than happy to relieve her of the responsibility and take over the mortgage for her. I'm sure it can be arranged without a signature from Mac.'

Ben knew Miles well enough to know he had no concern for Sarah. He wanted the ranch and he wanted it for pennies on the dollar. 'To be perfectly honest with you, Miles, a signature from Mac wouldn't be necessary. It so happens that Sarah owns the ranch, not Mac.'

Miles took a step back at this news. It took him completely by surprise. 'Sarah owns the Shepard ranch? When did this happen? Mac has owned the ranch for years. Why would he sell it to Sarah?'

'It happened before Mac disappeared. I don't know his reasons, Miles. But I know for a fact that Sarah is the owner of the Shepard ranch. If you've an interest in purchasing it, I suggest you take that up with her.'

'I might just do that,' replied Miles. 'Thanks for the information.' Miles gave Ben a good-natured pat on the shoulder as he continued on his way. The wheels were already turning as Miles began to devise a plan before he even finished talking to Ben.

Ben knew Miles was on a fool's errand. Sarah would never sell the ranch. It had already been promised to Jason.

When Ben returned to his office, he told Sarah about his encounter with Miles and warned her that he might be wanting to talk with her about buying the ranch. He suggested that she be ready. 'Miles can be pretty underhanded when he's after something he wants. I wouldn't be surprised if he does some research before he approaches you. I suggest we do some of our own. I know a few things about Miles that we can look into, just to be prepared.'

Sarah agreed and she and Ben began to prepare for the day Miles would approach her with his offer.

Miles, on the other hand, not knowing the full situation, thought he might have a chance at getting his hands on the Shepard ranch. He made a few discreet inquiries, to be sure Ben wasn't mistaken in his belief that Sarah owned the ranch. He wasn't. It seems Mac had signed over the deed to Sarah close to a year ago, but the papers were only filed several months ago. 'Why did she wait so long?' he wondered. 'Was she waiting for some word from Mac?' If that were the case, it could prove that Mac was still alive. Miles filed this information in his back pocket just in case he needed it later; after all, there still was the concern of foul play floating around out there. If Miles ever had to prove that Mac was indeed alive, this just might be it.

If she was reluctant, he might just bring this bit of information into the conversation. He thought he could take advantage of his misguided perception that she was a woman and incapable of handling the affairs of running the operation. He was hoping she was becoming emotionally overwhelmed with the hard decisions a ranch owner needed to make on a daily basis. It wasn't long before Miles decided to approach Sarah with an offer to buy the ranch.

If her answer was no, he would inform her that he knew Mac was still alive. If for her own private reasons she wanted to continue keeping it a secret, she would need to consider that, if he had to, he would expose the fact that not only did she know that Mac was alive, she most likely knew where he was hiding. Miles hoped that this might be the very thing that would cause her to decide in his favor. He obviously didn't know Sarah very well.

While Miles was devising his plan, Sarah and Ben were developing their own. Through his contacts in town, Ben was given access to written information concerning Miles and his most recent purchase of nearly five hundred acres of prime grazing land. It seems there was some discrepancy as to the actual ownership of the property he had purchased. Enough so, that it was heading for the courts to decide. But for some reason, it never made it that far. Seems the dispute was resolved out of court in favor of Miles soon after the judge in charge of the case received a rather large anonymous donation toward his upcoming re-election campaign. The speculation by those who claimed title to the land in question was that Miles had made the 'donation', but they had no way to prove it. The accusation was almost scandalous, but Miles was able somehow to get past it. Ben filled Sarah in on the details. 'Put this under your bonnet, and if Miles tries to pull some underhanded stunt on you, pull it out. It should be enough to shut him up,' stated Ben.

Sarah had little concern in her ability to handle Miles. Her confidence had grown tremendously over the past couple of years. She was almost looking forward to talking with him as she had grown to despise the man and would like nothing better than to put him in his place. Her opportunity came sooner than she expected.

It was several days later, about mid-morning, when Miles entered the doctor's office to find Sarah sitting at the reception desk. 'Just the woman I was looking for,' he stated. 'May I have a moment of your time?'

'Why, yes you may,' Sarah replied sweetly. She knew exactly what was on the man's mind, but she decided to play with him. 'Do you need to make an appointment?'

'Oh no,' replied Miles. 'I'd like to talk with you about a private matter.'

Sarah smiled. 'Shall we step outside?'

'That would be perfect,' replied Miles.

The two stepped outside and sat on the bench out front.

'What can I do for you, Miles?'

As usual, Miles got right to the point. 'Sarah, I have it on good authority that you, and not Mac, are the owner of the Shepard ranch, is that correct?'

'Yes, that would be true,' replied Sarah coldly.

Miles continued. 'As I'm sure you must know by now, with Mac being gone for as long as he has, that running an operation like the Shepard ranch is a very stressful proposition, don't you agree?'

'That would be true as well,' replied Sarah calmly.

Miles continued stating his case. 'Sarah, running a ranch as large as the Shepard is not the position a woman should find herself in, especially one who is already working a job. The stress will be too much for you. With Ben being as busy as he is, he won't be much help. I know Jason is doing his best, but let's face it, he's still young. He won't be able to handle things on his own for some time.'

'Miles, just what are you getting at here?' questioned Sarah. She knew what was coming next.

'I'm here to ask you, Sarah, if you would consider selling me the Shepard ranch?'

There it was. Plain, simple and to the point.

'Now let me get this straight,' replied Sarah. 'You think that because I'm a woman I should be frail and weak. That I should be over my head and full of undue stress. That running a ranch is no place for a woman. And that Jason is too young to take on the responsibility of day-to-day operations. Is that what you're saying?'

'Well,' Miles swallowed hard and tried to backpedal some. 'I'm not saying that it's impossible, just that, as a woman, you shouldn't have to. Sell the ranch to me and I'll make sure the Mac Shepard ranch is always productive and growing.'

'Miles, I appreciate your offer, but I think Jason and I will be able to handle the stress of running the ranch just fine.' Sarah stood to leave.

Miles was about to lose his only chance at owning the Shepard ranch, so he played his ace in the hole. 'Sarah, please sit back down and listen to what I have to say.'

Sarah obliged him and sat back down.

'Listen, I happen to know that Mac is still alive. I also know that you're aware of this as well. In fact, I'll venture to guess that you know exactly where he's hiding out. If that were to come out you could be charged with hiding a criminal and be required to tell the authorities where he is. I know you don't want that and your secret will remain safe with me, but only as long as you're willing to sell me the ranch. I tried to go about this nicely, but you give me no choice, so now I'm telling you how it is. Either you sell or I go to the sheriff with this information, and if I have to, I'll go above his head and get a real US Marshal involved. Is that what you want?'

Miles thought for sure Sarah would panic at the thought of being an accomplice and agree to the sale, but what he got in return was totally unexpected.

Sarah was surprised at what Miles had just told her, but she knew he hadn't a leg to stand on with his threat, and she didn't let it taint her reply. She stood up and leaned over Miles. She pointed an accusing finger at him as she began her caustic reply. 'Miles Hanley, you are an underhanded son-of-a-bitch.'

Miles was shocked to hear such language coming out of the mouth of a woman. He sat quietly as Sarah continued.

'If you think for one minute that I'm going to let you bully and blackmail me into selling my ranch to you, you're sadly mistaken. In fact, let me tell you a thing or two. I happen to know for a fact that the last land purchase you made was due to go to court to resolve a discrepancy concerning the title. Seems someone other than the seller was claiming owner-ship. It also sounds like they had good grounds, but for some, shall we say 'unknown' reasons, the case was dismissed. Rumor has it, and with good cause I might add, that the judge was bought off with a hand-some donation to his re-election campaign. Now this whole case can easily be brought back into the light of day, which includes the evidence I have on you. Is that what *you* want? If you're enjoying that five hundred acres, I suggest you crawl back under the rock you came out from and forget we ever had this conversation. That's the *only* deal you're going to get from me.'

Miles was dumbfounded. Sarah played her cards well. She had no real evidence. Miles only assumed she did.

He almost choked on his words as he forced them from his mouth. 'You are a formidable woman, Sarah. I never would have expected this from you. Never. I must admit, you've trumped me. You can consider this conversation done and forgotten.' Miles stood up and tipped his hat. 'You have a good day, ma'am.' He stepped off the boardwalk and walked down the street like an old dog that had just been scolded.

Sarah stepped back inside. The smile on her face said it all. She couldn't wait for Ben to return so she could recount the whole conversation to him. He would certainly be proud.

Miles had learned a thing or two about Sarah that day and he never brought the subject up again.

CHAPTER 9

THE LAST TEMPTATION

With each passing day, Jason could feel the life he wanted to live slipping from his grasp. He didn't mind the hard work, and he loved the sense of accomplishment he felt at the end of each day, but the idea of doing the same thing in this one spot for the rest of his life held very little appeal to his adventurous nature. He was still a young man and the thought of settling down at such an early age was hard to take. Maybe he would be more inclined to give up the idea in a few years, but he hadn't reached that point yet.

It was early in the fall and a Friday night. Jason

needed a break from the ranch and decided to head into town with his two hired men. They headed to the Hoof and Horn for a couple of drinks and a hand or two of cards.

They had been there about an hour. Jason was standing at the bar talking with Ira, the bartender, when a stranger walked through the door and up to the bar. Jason kept quiet as the man ordered a drink. The stranger had a very heavy Southern accent. He looked to be in his mid-thirties; his clothes were too fancy for him to be a regular hand unless of course he had dressed up for the occasion of coming into the Hoof and Horn, which seemed very unlikely. The giveaway was that he didn't carry his gun like a regular ranch hand might. It hung low on his hip, which would enable him to make a quick draw if necessary. He lit up a thin, store-bought cigar.

Card shark or gun fighter, thought Jason as the stranger picked up his drink and walked over to an empty table where he took a seat and focused his attention on a group of men at the next table playing cards.

'What do you think, Ira?' asked Jason in a low voice.

'Not sure,' Ira replied. 'With an accent like that I can tell you one thing for sure, he's definitely not from around here.'

'You're right about that, Ira,' agreed Jason.

'There's something about this guy, I'm not sure what it is, but he intrigues me. I think I'll strike up a conversation with him and find out exactly where he came from and just what he's up to.' He gave Ira a smile as he picked up his bottle and a glass.

'You should leave the questioning to the sheriff,' commented Ira as Jason headed toward the stranger. 'You watch yourself,' he added.

Jason set the bottle and his glass on the table and introduced himself. 'How do you do. My name's Jason. Care for some company?'

The stranger was sitting easy in his chair. He looked up at Jason. Removed the cigar from his mouth and flicked the ashes on to the floor. 'Are y'all someone I should know?' he asked with his heavy southern drawl.

'Not necessarily,' replied Jason. 'It's Saturday night and I'm offering you a drink. No more to it than that.'

The stranger motioned for Jason to sit down. 'A man with a bottle is always welcome at my table. Name's Tanner, Caleb Tanner. If y'all have anything to do with the law around here, I'll tell you now, my friend and I are just passing through.'

'I'm not the law. Who's your friend?' questioned Jason. 'Are you referring to the gun on your hip?'

Tanner laughed. 'Oh hell no, son. That thing is nothing more than the bane of my existence, it mostly keeps me out of trouble and occasionally gets me into it. My friend I refer to is out back relieving himself as we speak. He'll be about shortly.'

Just as Tanner finished his sentence, a voice from behind Jason spoke up. 'I see you've met Tanner?'

Jason turned to see his old friend, Wes, standing behind him.

'Well I'll be damned.' Jason stood and grabbed up the hand of his old friend. 'Wes. How the hell are you? How have you been? *Where* have you been?'

Wes took a seat. 'I've been doing well for myself. Spent some time down in Texas and then made my way to Mississippi. That's where I picked up this stray.' Wes pointed in Tanner's direction.

'Don't let him fool you,' interjected Tanner jokingly. 'I fairly won this northerner in a poker game. He's my slave for the next year.'

Wes shot back. 'Oh bullshit, you lying sack a . . .'

Tanner interrupted once again. 'You know it's true, son. You only brought me this far north hoping someone would take offense to the fact that I'm a true Southerner, and put a bullet in me so you'll be relieved of the debt.' Tanner flicked his ashes and smiled widely.

The two continued their jovial bantering until Wes could see he wasn't going to get the upper hand, so he changed the subject. 'So, Jason, tell me, what have you been up to? The last time I saw you, Miles Hanley had just fired you from the XO. That really pissed me off, you know. That's the day I decided to quit that outfit. It was the best thing I ever did.'

Jason talked about how he had traveled down to Texas before heading back to Kansas and how he was now running the Shepard ranch. He did leave out the details as to why Mac had left him in charge.

'So your pa left town and left you in charge of his ranch, just like that?' questioned Wes, snapping his fingers.

'Yeah, pretty much, he was tired of trying to make it work. Said he wasn't cut out to be a rancher and wanted to do some traveling. It'll be mine, but not for a couple more years. He thought I might like to try my hand at it. If I make a go of it and want to continue, he'll turn it over to me when I turn twenty-one. To be perfectly honest, I'm not so sure about being a rancher myself. Your life on the trail is exactly what I'd really like to be doing right about now.'

Tanner had been sitting quietly as the two men talked. He kept himself occupied by inconspicuously flirting with a couple of the saloon girls. He eventually spoke up, directing his comments toward Jason. 'Why hell, son. We're not planning to stay here long. Why don't you unburden yourself from this ranch business you so hate and come with us. You never know, I may need someone to watch my back on the way out of town.'

Jason didn't answer directly. He took a deep breath as he contemplated his reply. 'You know, Tanner, I'd love to take you up on that, but I can't, I have a ranch to run.' As he spoke those words he felt them cut at him like a knife through the heart. 'I can't just *unburden*,' he stressed the word, 'myself and up and leave. It's not that simple.' Jason almost felt sick to his stomach as he spoke those words.

Tanner looked at Jason. He leaned forward; pulled the cigar from his mouth and jabbed it toward Jason as he spoke. 'Son, I can surely see that you are a man in distress. Let me tell you something. All my life I've made my living at the table. I played for the house on a Mississippi river boat, and I made damn good money for myself and my employer. Now I make a damn good living on my own. Point is, I play the game well because I know how to read a man. I know what he's thinking, I believe I can see into a man's very soul, and as for you son, I see you as being shackled against your will. You hate every minute of it and would love nothing more than to find a way to break free. I'm telling you, there are always excuses for not doing a thing. Sometimes you got to dig deep and find the courage to break free. Throw yourself into the wind like Wes and I. Let it grab you up and just go wherever it takes you. That's freedom, son, that's freedom.'

He put the cigar back into his mouth and puffed

on it with assurance as he leaned back in his chair.

'Tanner, it's not as easy as you make it sound.' replied Jason, 'I'd love to just throw myself into the wind, I really would, but I can't. I've got cows to feed.'

'Well, we all got somewhere to be and somethin' to do, now don't we,' replied Tanner.

Jason had heard enough. He stood up and reached across the table to shake hands with Tanner and Wes. 'It was nice to meet you, Tanner, and good to see you again, Wes. I'm glad we ran into each other. Why don't the two of you stop by the ranch on your way out?'

'We will,' replied Wes.

Tanner wasn't so sure. 'We will, if the wind is in your favor,' he replied.

Jason considered Tanner's answer as he walked out the door into the cool night air. A slight breeze was beginning to blow as he mounted his horse. The ride back toward the ranch was slow, as Jason wrestled with his feelings of discontent along the way. Jason decided not to head home that night. Instead, he veered off the trail toward a solitary place he had frequented in the past. At times like this when he felt the world was closing in on him, this was the place he would seek out, kindle a fire and camp out under the stars. He would lay his head back on his saddle and gaze upon the starry night sky as he contemplated his place in the world. Tonight was one of those nights. He had to make some major decisions before he found himself stuck in place. He only hoped it wasn't too late.

The stars were comforting and the fire was warm, but even so, Jason was restless and didn't sleep well. It was a cool night and the morning didn't come soon enough. He rekindled the fire before the sun had come up and warmed his bones as he made his peace with his demons. For now, he was stuck and he knew it, so he would make the best of it. Somehow he needed to turn over a new leaf and start fresh. An idea had come to him during the night and he planned to act upon it that very morning. He was hungry and in want of a hot cup of coffee, so he saddled up, but he didn't continue on to the ranch. Jason headed back to town. As he rode in he happened to see Wes and Tanner riding out. They were heading in the opposite direction. He let them go without so much as a holler. He rode past the saloon and hitched his horse in front of the barbershop.

The barber was just finishing up with a customer and no one else was in the shop as Jason walked in.

'Well, if it ain't Jason McKinney,' commented the barber. 'You've walked by my shop a hundred times, but never once have you darkened my door. What can I do for you this morning?'

'I'd like a haircut, Frank,' Jason replied.

Frank almost dropped his razor as he heard Jason's request.

'Son, do you know how long I've been wanting to get a hold of that mop of yours? This is a day to remember, yessiree, a day to remember. You just sit yourself right down here in this chair and let's get to it.'

Jason took a seat. 'Cut it short,' he ordered. 'Make me look respectable.'

'You got it. In fact, for this momentous occasion, I'm going to throw in a shave at no charge. Yessiree, this here is a momentous occasion.'

Once Frank had finished his work, he held out a mirror for Jason to examine the results. 'Well, what do you think?'

'Well,' replied Jason. 'I sure look different. I've never had my hair this short, but I guess I'll get used to it. You did a good job.'

Jason paid for the haircut and grabbed up his hat. He put it on and it fell over his eyes. Jason just stood there as Frank broke out into a hearty laugh. 'Looks like you need a new hat,' he jested.

'I think you're right,' Jason replied.

He took off the hat and walked next door to the mercantile where he bought a brand new one, and a new shirt to boot.

His next stop would be the bath house, where he could soak off several days' worth of sweat and trail dust.

After his bath, Jason was mighty hungry, and the thought of a good breakfast and hot coffee was heavy on his mind. Being a Saturday, he decided to ride over to Ben and Sarah's new house and surprise them. He'd get his breakfast there.

He rode out feeling pretty good about the day and soon arrived at the gate. Jason hitched his horse and walked up to the front door. Not wanting to just walk in, he knocked and waited until Sarah opened it. Sarah had to do a double take. She looked at Jason as if she didn't recognize him for a second or two. She started to greet the stranger with a 'Good morning, what can . . .' then the recognition came. Her face lit up and she smiled from ear to ear. 'Jason, is that you?' she knowingly asked. 'I almost didn't recognize you. Come in. What are you doing in town? Let me get a good look at you.' Sarah stepped back and examined him up and down. 'My, you're a mighty handsome man,' she exclaimed.

Just then Ben walked into the room. 'What's all the commotion?' he questioned as he stepped up to Sarah. Seeing Jason took him by surprise. 'Well look at you. A haircut and clean clothes even. You look like you're heading to church or something. Did you get religion?'

Jason laughed. 'No, Ben, not religion. Just a new attitude about life. If I'm going to be a ranch owner, I need to start acting like one. I'm working on getting more responsible and respectable, *and* I'm also hoping to get some coffee and breakfast.'

'Well you've come to the right place,' replied Sarah. 'Let's head into the kitchen.'

'We have a new cook and she makes the best darn hotcakes I've ever eaten,' commented Ben. 'Much better than those darned old saddle blankets the last cook made.'

'They weren't *that* bad,' replied Sarah. 'At any rate, we have hot coffee on the stove and the new cook is here today. We haven't eaten yet ourselves. I'll introduce her to you.'

The three of them walked into the kitchen. The new cook was busily working over the stove. She had her back to them. As they entered, she turned and swiped the hair from her face with her forearm and wiped her hands on her apron.

Sarah introduced her. 'Susan, looks like we have one more for breakfast. I'd like you to meet my son, Jason.'

Susan held out her hand to Jason. Her hair was long and brown, she was about Jason's age and had the features of a full-grown woman. Jason took her hand and couldn't help but notice how strikingly beautiful she was. He also noticed there was no ring on her finger.

'Glad to meet you, Jason,' she answered. 'Please call me Sue.'

Their eyes met and they held each other's gaze for what seemed like longer than normal. Jason found her smile to be intoxicating.

Sarah interrupted. 'Susan and her parents just recently moved here from Missouri.'

'Well I'm very glad to meet you,' replied Jason as he let go of her hand.

After some small talk they walked out to the dining room. Jason turned to get one more glimpse of Sue. She caught his glance and gave him a bright smile.

As Jason continued to the table he thought to himself. *This may not be such a long winter after all.*